HURRICANE

Andrew Salkey

HURRICANE

London
OXFORD UNIVERSITY PRESS

Oxford University Press, Ely House, London W. 1

GLASGOW   NEW YORK   TORONTO   MELBOURNE   WELLINGTON
CAPE TOWN   SALISBURY   IBADAN   NAIROBI   DAR ES SALAAM   LUSAKA   ADDIS ABABA
BOMBAY   CALCUTTA   MADRAS   KARACHI   LAHORE   DACCA
KUALA LUMPUR   SINGAPORE   HONG KONG   TOKYO

First published 1964
Reprinted 1968, 1969
First published in this edition 1971

Reprinted 1976

TO

Eliot and Jason

Printed in Holland
Zuid-Nederlandsche Drukkerij N.V.
's-Hertogenbosch

CONTENTS

Year in, year out, the land looks up and waits.
Year in, year out, the land is battered by the slanting rain,
Which softens the brain, the earth, rots the sugar cane,
Washes away the top soil, breeds angry mosquitoes.
The land is flattened by hurricanes, like pneumatic drills,
Which uproot ancient trees, smash houses,
Splinter the sleepers on railway tracks,
Whiten the corners of hungry mouths,
And drown the population, given half a chance.

From a poem by a Jamaican poet

PROLOGUE

1

Although my name is really Joseph Nathaniel Brown, my parents and all my friends call me Joe for short.

I was named after my father, who, by the way, is a contractor and builder. My sister, Mary, was named after my mother, who is a dressmaker.

Mary is nine and I am four years older.

2

I like telling stories. I also like writing them down. I have decided to write about the exciting time I once had during a hurricane which blew through the whole Island and which caused a lot of damage to a large portion of Kingston and Saint Andrew.

At that time, we were all living in an old-fashioned wooden house on Orange Street just below Torrington Bridge.

Funnily enough, only a few months before the hurricane, Mama and Papa had begun to make plans to move to a new house on Tuna Avenue in Harbour View.

And, strange as it may seem, on the morning of the hurricane, Mary and I had secretly hoped that the time would soon come for us to go to our Aunt Maud in Westmoreland to spend part of our summer holidays.

The month was August.

PART ONE
MORNING

1

Mary and I have been on our summer holidays for about five weeks now. Nothing very much has happened so far, but we have planned to do all sorts of things when we go down to Westmoreland to spend time with Aunt Maud, who is our father's sister.

Aunt Maud is our favourite aunt. She has always been more than an aunt to us. In fact, sometimes we think of her as a big sister. The things we remember most of all about her are her deep-set, darting eyes, her very dry sense of humour, her tall, thin body, and her fantastic energy and courage when everything around her seems to be going against her.

When I got up this morning, I overheard my father saying to my mother: 'Yes, I know, Mary love, holidays are holidays and children are only young once, but August can be a wicked month—you know that. If it isn't a cloud-burst, it's a storm. If it isn't a storm, it's a hurricane. That's why I don't think we should send Joe and Mary to the country at all. We can always write to Maud and explain.'

My father might sound as though he is on the side of the storm and the hurricane, but my mother is usually on our side. I heard her say: 'Just because the Meteorological Office printed a hand-out about tropical storms after the last cloud-burst some years ago and because the same Met. people published a little warning in the *Gleaner* about a breeze-blow this month, you're more than ready now to stop the children from going down to the country to enjoy themselves. The warning never said a thing about a *deluge* in Westmoreland, you know.'

'I never said anything about a deluge, either,' Papa objected. 'Don't mix me up with Noah and the Old Testament at all.'

Mama laughed her usual sarcastic laugh and said, 'Cho, man! Even old Noah in the Bible was calmer than you. What I want to know is why a grown man like you must start worrying about something that may never happen? In any case, we can't disappoint Joe and Mary because you're being your usual self, believing every little thing you hear, and giving in to your own personal fears and anxiety. After all, Joe and Mary have been waiting patiently for five weeks now.'

'No!' Papa said. '*No* Maud and *no* Westmoreland. Joe and Mary are going to stay right here in Kingston where I can keep an eye on them for their own good.'

'And where you can keep an eye on the Met. Office, I suppose?' Mama suggested.

'And on that as well,' Papa said, laughing softly.

As a matter of fact, I'm sure Mama expected Papa to laugh. She laughed too.

2

Because it was Saturday, Mama had promised to let us go to the morning show at Carib Theatre. So, after our favourite breakfast of *ackee,* salt fish, hard dough bread, pear, and country chocolate, Mary and I decided to walk across to the Race Course and wander around for a while until it was time to go back home and dress for the pictures.

On our way to the Race Course, Mary said, 'So it looks as if we're not going to spend time with Aunt Maud after all.'

'You heard them talking, then?' I asked, surprised that she actually had.

I was hoping to keep the conversation between Mama and Papa a secret from her. I didn't want to upset her first thing in the morning.

''Course I did,' Mary said, pouting a little. 'I heard every word they said.'

'Maybe Papa'll change his mind later on,' I said, trying to cheer her up, but she shrugged her shoulders and chirped her teeth.

I honestly don't think she did so out of rudeness but because she was feeling down in the mouth at the time. Mary is like that, you know. When she is disappointed, she really takes it to heart and at the same time she tries her best to show that she doesn't care a row of pins. But I know she does.

'Think there's going to be a hurricane, Joe?' she asked.

'No, man,' I said quickly, realizing that there was nothing else for me to say, 'a shower of rain, perhaps, but definitely not a hurricane.'

Of course, I had my doubts, especially after listening to what Papa had said about the month of August, and what Mama had said about the Met. Office hand-out and the report in the *Gleaner*.

I looked at Mary and was just in time to see her lowering her eyes, her chin still pointing upwards.

'Looking at the clouds won't help you,' I said.

'That's a downright lie and you know it,' she said angrily.

'All right, Mary, so I've been fooling you,' I told her, trying all I could to pass it off as a joke. 'Those black clouds up there mean one thing: big trouble later on. There's going to be the most *terrific* hurricane of all time. In about ten minutes, in fact.'

I laughed just to prove I wasn't being serious. I even made a funny face, lolled out my tongue, stuck my thumbs in my ears and fanned out my fingers.

But Mary turned and stared through me—or so it seemed.

'Listen,' she said, pointing to the entrance of a general hardware store which stocks electrical appliances and stuff like that.

I turned round.

'Hear that, Joe?'

'Hear what?' I asked.

'The radio.'

I listened.

Mary took my hand, and we walked back a little way towards the entrance of the store.

The radio announcer was saying: ' . . . will be overcast. So far, high winds are expected, together with intermittent showers which might become heavy and continuous in the late afternoon.'

There was a pause and then music.

'Late afternoon?' I asked Mary.

'It's the hurricane,' she said and started to walk away from me.

She was walking so quickly that I had to run to catch up with her.

We held hands and entered the Race Course. For quite a long time we said nothing to each other and kept looking in different directions and thinking our own separate thoughts.

The morning was very hot. Our hands were warm and sticky. Everywhere we went there were wide shimmering waves of heat, flowing across the stunted grass and seeming all the time to be always at an even distance in front of us.

I like walking about in the Race Course. I like the bigness of the place, the hill-and-gully feeling of the ground under my feet, the hardness of the scattered stones, the stifled, crunchy sounds of the loose pebbles, the pretty patchwork pattern of ram-goat roses, buttercups, and shame-lady vines. I even like the old grandstand and the rusty railings and pieces of twisted iron lying about. But, in a way, everything seemed slightly changed now. Walking slowly beside Mary and not talking or anything made it even worse. In fact, I began to hate the place, to tell the truth. All of a sudden, I wanted to run and wave my hands about and shout. I wanted to run out into the street and take a bus, any bus, or stop a car or fling a stone at something or do anything but walk as I was doing with Mary. She must have been reading my thoughts at that moment because she let go of my hand and asked, 'Want to run a little, Joe? You always do when we get to this spot.'

'Yes, I wouldn't mind a sprint,' I said, beginning to limber up with a few knee-lifts.

'Run then,' Mary said. 'I'll wait here for you.'

She sat down and turned her face away towards Wolmer's Boys' School.

I broke into a sprint, imagining that I was running a fantastic hundred yards dash at Championships at Sabina Park, but after about sixty yards or so I checked my speed and cruised down to the tape, cool and easy, and kept going long after I had passed it. I must have done more than a 'two-twenty' when I suddenly got fed up and started walking back to Mary. I felt foolish running off and leaving her sitting on her own. I felt she felt that I was foolish to have done so.

When I got back, she said, 'Should've told you not to, Joe.'

'Not to what?' I asked.

'Not to run right after eating,' she said casually.

She got up, stretched her arms wide above her head, and yawned long and loud.

Gosh, boy! The heat was blazing now—not a glimpse of the sun, just a sort of grey flannel blanket over everything.

In a way, you know, I like the setting very much. Out on the Race Course, it's like a real fabulous prairie, when you come to think about it: *and then,* five cowboys appear over the horizon. They come riding in, nice and easy. All of a sudden, they start to put on their black handkerchiefs up to their eyes. Then they pat their holsters to see if their guns are in place. After that, they look around for the star of the film, who is a famous Dodge City gun-slinger turned Sheriff.

I mean to say: the setting is perfect for an action-packed Western. Dead right!

And the background music is going on all the while, building up slowly and grinding away on your nerves, until the hero rides in from the opposite direction, stops a little way off, and says, 'O.K., Rango, so far and no farther. Just turn round again and head back East.'

And before anybody can bat an eyelid, Rango flashes a quick draw on the Sheriff and says—

'If we're going to the pictures, we'd better go back home now, Joe,' Mary reminded me.

I laughed quietly to myself and nodded.

Poor Sheriff.

8

Papa had gone out when we got back. Mama was working at her sewing-machine. The radio was on.

'Your father just phoned to tell both of you not to bother to go to Carib today,' Mama said. She did not even look up at us. Her feet were pedalling frantically and her hands were guiding the dress-material round and about the plunging needle.

Mary grinned. I didn't know what to do. I just stood and waited.

'You understand the message?' Mama asked. '*No* pictures today.'

'Why?' I asked.

'Because he says that somebody told him that the Met. people have just sent up a plane to plot the course of the storm, or something like that,' Mama chuckled.

'What does "plot" mean?' Mary asked, as I knew she would.

Mama looked at me as much as to say, 'I have enough worries as it is. You tell her, Joe.'

So I said, 'It means trying to find out exactly where the storm is blowing, the direction it's likely to follow, its force, speed, size and shape and that sort of thing, I suppose.'

'So there *is* going to be a hurricane then?' Mary said.

'Your father and the Met. people seem to think so,' Mama said.

'And the radio too,' Mary added.

'The radio can think most anything it wants to turn its mind to, child,' Mama said, laughing her sarcastic laugh.

'So, no pictures then?' I asked.

Mama pretended not to hear. I repeated my question. No answer. Instead, she made the sewing-machine hum the loudest I'd heard for ages.

Mary sat down and smiled. She had caught on.

'In any case, I'm not going,' she said.

I put my question to Mama for the third time.

'All right, Joe,' she said, taking her feet off the pedal and turning round to face me, 'I don't think there's going to be any cloud-burst, breeze-blow, storm, or hurricane. I don't think there's going to be an earthquake either. I don't even think the Devil and his wife are going to fight, if you really want to know.' She sighed like a tired teacher and said, 'Yes, Joe, go to Carib.'

4

Carib was as empty as King Street on a Sunday morning. You could have chased a rat through the whole place and caught it with the greatest of ease.

It's true that I saw a few friends from school and a few from my street, but the usual crowd just wasn't there at all. 'Four Eyes' Dodd was nowhere in sight. Neither were 'Pants' Martin, 'Jiji-Wappie' Haughton, 'Moon Face' Smith, 'Popeye' Mason, nor 'Shaved Head' Chin. Frankly, these were the boys that actually made the morning show a great thing: for instance, while the picture was going on, 'Four Eyes' would help out the sound-track by supplying background music when there wasn't any; 'Pants' would shoot louder than any of the cowboys or gangsters on the screen; 'Jiji-Wappie' would always laugh in the wrong places in every single film we saw; 'Moon Face' would be the first to start shouting encouraging remarks to the star of the film if things were going badly for him; 'Popeye' would shadow-box every time there was a fight, and quite often he would slap a *full-nelson* on the boy sitting in front of him; and as for 'Shaved Head', well—he was the original cry-baby. 'Shaved Head' has been known to cry during a cartoon film.

So, you see, Carib wasn't going to be the same this morning.

Anyway, Milton Perkins, our brainly boy, 'B.B.', as we all call him, came up to me and announced like a real wise man: 'There's definitely going to be a brute of a hurricane, Joe. The wind's going to be anything up to sixty or eighty miles an hour, boy.'

Our 'B.B.' is a fantastic arithmetic genius, you know. He must have been up in the Met. plane.

I listened while he almost talked the hurricane into existence. Then I said to him: 'B.B., tell me something: how is it that your parents actually allowed you to come to Carib if this McKinley-Rhoden-Wint hurricane is really going to blow us all to kingdom-come?'

'Well, Joe, the position is like this: nobody at home knows about it yet, you understand, and I happen to know that things won't start to pop until late tonight. Get me?'

I got him all right. So I said, 'You must've worked it out for yourself, like a big time arithmetic sum, B.B.'

I watched his brainy face closely.

'Cho, man! The thing's as clear as day,' he said, putting his hands into his pockets.

I wanted to remind him that the day wasn't clear at all, but I didn't have the heart to interrupt good old B.B. Einstein.

'You see, Joe,' he continued, 'the facts speak for themselves. The whole thing is this: first of all, there's August for a start—you know what August, September, and October usually bring; then there's the report in the *Gleaner,* and that report is also another fact; the Met. people can't be wrong, or at least, they can't be too far out in their calculations; the radio is bound to have got the information from the Met. Office; and, apart from everything else, I have a book on the subject.'

'And your parents don't know a thing about all this?'

'You mean: about the hurricane tonight?'

'Yes.'

B.B. shook his head and said, 'Saterday is their day off, man. They're still sleeping. From last night.'

Just then, the theme music started, and B.B. left me and walked down the centre aisle. He had a lot of seats to choose from, both upstairs and downstairs. And so had I.

5

It was very, very hot when I left Carib. Although the traffic at Cross Roads was heavy and there were other noises as well, there was a sort of hush in the air. It made me feel that all the sounds around were locked in a big box and pushed far away from me.

I glimpsed B.B. and waved to him.

'Tonight!' he said, putting his hands to his ears and bending forwards as if to protect himself from some sort of on-coming rush of something or other.

'You've got water on the brain, B.B.!' I shouted back at him.

He straightened up, said, 'I've worked it out, boy,' and be-gan running towards the Carib back-entrance which led to Brentford Road.

On my way down Slipe Road, I saw Mother Samuel preaching to a small, silent crowd.

Mother Samuel is a tall, shabby old woman who thinks of herself as a modern prophet. She walks about the streets of Kingston and Saint Andrew, night and day, and tells everybody to repent because the end of the world is at hand.

Lots of people make fun of her. Girls are usually slightly afraid of her when she walks near to them. But boys, like

Four Eyes, Pants, and the rest, aren't.

Papa smiles when Mary and I mention Mother Samuel's name at home. Mama sighs and says, 'Poor woman.'

I don't mind Mother Samuel. As a matter of fact, I like her. I think she's lonely nearly all the time: that's why she has to walk around and warn everybody. I'm sure she does so because she knows that people will notice her, even though they give her a rough time.

As I got closer to the crowd, I heard her saying, 'The entire population of this wicked Island of ours is going to perish by hurricane at midnight tonight. Be advised by me and repent your sins before the hour comes to claim you all. Repent, sinners, big and small! Repent and be prepared to face your Maker!'

A man said, 'Mother, the hurricane can't just take us alone —what about the rest of the sinners all over the world?'

'Don't be a mocker, son,' Mother Samuel told him. 'I've been prophesying many things, including Armageddon, for many years now, but tonight is our turn to perish by water, not by the sword. The world will end tomorrow at midday, anyway, and not by water but by fire.'

Needless to say, I didn't believe Mother Samuel, but I was glad that Mary was not with me. I'm sure she would have believed every word.

I got into the centre of the crowd, folded my arms, and waited to hear more.

Mother Samuel was holding a banner which was nailed to a long slender stick. Written on the top half of the banner, in red paint which seemed to me to be wet and smudgy, were the words: WE DIE BY ORDER OF THE ALMIGHTY. WE DIE AS SINNERS IF WE DIE WITHOUT REPENTING.

She lifted the banner by its stick and slammed it down every now and again on the pavement as she continued her high-pitched warning.

'Mind you don't crack your voice, Mother!' a girl shouted from the back of the crowd. 'Things are thin as they are already.'

'The hurricane will blow it away before I can crack it,' Mother Samuel said. 'You sound like a student. You come from Mona, child?'

The girl said yes.

'Well,' Mother Samuel told her, 'you'd better go right back to Mona and do your last homework. Your Maker will mark it in heaven, if you repent. If you don't, the Devil will.'

Everybody laughed. So did Mother Samuel.

I left after that.

I walked down the right-hand side of the road, and all sorts of thoughts came into my head: I thought of Aunt Maud; I remembered Papa's voice saying: '*No* Maud and *no* Westmoreland'; I heard Mama's sewing-machine humming like an angry swarm of bees; I also heard the Met. plane searching for the hurricane; I saw Rango shooting it out with the Sheriff; I also saw Mother Samuel going up to heaven; then I saw B.B. working out the longest sum in the world.

Suddenly, all my thoughts began to run helter-skelter and they got so mixed up with one another that I had to force myself to stop my day-dreaming. Even though I was walking on Slipe Road and I was wide awake, those few minutes were exactly like the out-of-this-world feeling you get when you're just about dropping off to sleep at night. I had to shake myself to come back to reality.

I was sweating. I opened my shirt down to the third button and blew hard on my wet skin. Even my own breath was like the outside air; in fact, it was as hot.

I began walking quickly. I wanted to get home before Papa did. I wasn't thinking of pretending that I had not been to Carib; I simply wanted to be at home with Mama and Mary when he got in. In any case, I had had Mama's permission,

14

and I knew she would tell him that I had gone to the pictures. Of course, I wasn't sure what he'd say to her about it, but I imagined that he'd be annoyed with me, and perhaps, a little bit, too, with Mama.

Anyhow, I was covering the distance nicely. Then, just as I was passing a furniture store which had its radio turned up high, I heard the announcer saying: '. . . naturally there's no cause for alarm, but it's advisable to make an early start. Everybody, in the Corporate Area and out in the country, should begin immediately to take the usual precautions. I repeat: there's no cause for alarm. Make an early start and please take the usual precautions.'

There was a very slight pause.

Then he said: 'It is twelve o'clock precisely.'

PART TWO

AFTERNOON

1

Everything was all right when I got home. Mama and Mary were busy preparing our lunch of pumpkin soup, beef balls and white rice, and Papa had not yet come in. Of course, he had phoned Mama about the latest radio-announcement and had asked her to see about getting certain things ready for him. In a way, we are lucky that Papa is in the building trade; it means that we have quite a few useful things about the house, things like nails, bolts, staples, flat pieces of tin and zinc-sheeting, cording, rope, strips of pitch-pine board, and so on. All these were going to be used in one way and another later on, and I knew that Papa was expecting me to help him with the precautions which the radio announcer had talked about. The thing is: I had not actually heard them. Anyway, Papa had given Mama a list of duties which all of us had to help him to do when he got in.

Mama looked slightly worried. I thought that possibly she was coming round slowly to the fact that there was going to be a hurricane after all. She had not said so, but I had a sneaking feeling that the odds were against her. She was very quiet all the time and she moved about the house as if the place were not hers.

Mary was the same. She hardly spoke to me at all. However, she did mention that Mama had told Papa on the phone that I had gone to Carib, and she said that he'd told Mama that he hoped that I would have the good sense to come straight home afterwards. Mary also said that Papa hadn't talked much about the matter, and therefore she felt that things were, more or less, all right.

Mama handed me Papa's list and told me to collect the items on it without turning his work-room upside down. The list was not half as long as I had expected; the duties were many, though. In any case, I knew that he'd be bringing home a lot of other things to eke out what he already had.

Mary gave me a very funny look when Mama handed me the list, and I knew that something was wrong somehow, but I promised myself to ask her about it later.

I like Papa's work-room, which, incidentally, is tucked away at the back of the house. It's like a hobbies exhibition in a store moved right into your own home. Of course, Papa doesn't allow me to use his equipment and he dislikes any of us being near him, even outside the door, when he's working on a job in the nights or on Sundays. I think the best thing about the room is the way everything is fitted up and set out: there is a large variety of tools and fixtures on three walls; on the fourth, there are cupboards and a number of builders' plans and carpenters' work-diagrams stuck with sellotape; and there are electrical gadgets in three corners and a big dustbin in the fourth.

As soon as I went into the room, I began to rummage about

17

in the wood-shavings on the floor. Then I looked aimlessly in all the wall-cupboards. However, when I began to search properly, I found a large box of three-inch nails, many lumps of plasterers' putty wrapped in grease-proof paper, several narrow pieces of pitch-pine cut in varying lengths, two huge rolls of canvas, and other odds and ends.

Beside the dustbin in the corner nearest the door, I found a chocolate box filled with an assortment of glistening ball-bearings. I had just taken one out to look at it when Mary walked in and sat down on the work-table in the centre of the room. She stared at me and began to shake her legs, a bad habit which Mama and Papa have been trying, for ages, to make her stop.

'What's the matter?' I asked, quickly and quietly dropping the ball-bearing back into the box and turning round casually and frowning at her.

Honestly, I hate people who come into a room, catch you doing something private and personal, and just sit and stare at you.

She didn't answer me.

'Didn't you hear me?' I asked, frowning even harder. 'What's the matter?'

'Nothing,' she said, jumping off the table and landing awkwardly on a pile of wood-shavings.

'How d'you mean *nothing*?' I asked, walking over to her like a no-nonsense sheriff who's about to prove that he's the fastest gun in town.

'Joe,' she said, narrowing her eyes and clasping her hands behind her neck, 'what d'you think you're doing?'

'Collecting the things Papa wants, of course.'

'They aren't going to be of any use, you know, Silly Billy.'

'Why aren't they going to be useful, Miss Meddlesome Matty?' I felt like drawing my Forty-Five and letting her have it.

'Because the wind and the rain are going to be too strong.

18

That's why.'

'That's what you think,' I said confidently. 'Anyway, Papa and I know better.'

Now I understood why she had looked at me the way she had when Mama first handed me the list.

'You, Papa, those nails, and all those pieces of pitch-pine can't even stop a runaway donkey-cart much more a hurricane, so don't try to tell me that you and Papa *know* better.'

She frowned.

At that moment, I really felt like letting her have it straight between the eyes from where I was standing, but I reckoned that a sheriff can't be a Law Man and a Bad Man all at the same time; besides, Mary's a girl who has just come in on a Wells Fargo stage-coach. I had to be a real sheriff and take care of her.

I smiled a little and bent down over the box of nails which was between us. She kicked it playfully towards me and said, 'What film did you see?'

I told her the title.

She asked me to tell her the story.

I did so briefly.

When I came to the end of it, she said softly, as though she hadn't been listening to me at all, and with tears beginning to well up in her eyes, 'Joe, is it going to be really bad? Will it wash us all away? Are we going to die, Joe?'

I hugged her, took her over to the corner, and showed her the chocolate box of glistening ball-bearings.

2

Papa came home just as Mama was about to serve lunch. He kissed her cheek, and she put her hand up to her forehead and said, 'I know it's a bad thing to say, but it's only a hurri-

19

cane that can get you to come home on time for your lunch.'

Papa smiled, held Mary's shoulder and mine, leant over us, and said, 'Don't listen to your Mother, you hear. She's the best cook in the world. Only a fool wouldn't be on time for her cooking.'

Mama placed her arms akimbo and said, 'So you're calling yourself a fool then? And a real old-time one at that.'

After we had eaten, Papa looked at the clock on the sideboard, asked for his list, and read it through slowly.

It was a little after half past one.

The radio had been turned off. Papa got up and switched it on and then sat down beside it.

Mary soon became restless. Mama called her into the kitchen and started up the usual sort of women's talk they often go in for when Papa and I are otherwise occupied about the house.

'I saw a lot of Red Cross people and emergency volunteers going into Coke Chapel, son,' Papa said, tapping his fingers on the dial of the radio.

'Why Coke Chapel, Papa?' I asked, drawing up my chair next to his.

'It's as good a relief centre as any,' he said, turning down the volume of sound. 'Temporary measures, son. Anyway, some buildings are stronger than others. I suppose other centres are being fixed up right now.'

'But what's going to go on in them?'

'At the moment, only preparations, I'd imagine, stocking up of drugs, blankets, old clothes if any are handy, making bandages, and that sort of thing. Later they might have a soup-kitchen set up somewhere near the centres, and so on. Depends on how bad things are after the hurricane, of course.'

'What about the Met. Office, Papa?'

'Ought to be very busy, son.'

'And the plane?'

20

'I don't know, but I'd imagine it's still up. Mind you, they may have recalled it and sent up another. I really don't know.'

We were silent for a few moments. Then I asked, 'Are we going to start our precautions now, Papa?'

He looked at me for a while, his eyes staring dreamily through me, and said, 'Yes, son. In a minute. I want to hear the latest before we go outside.'

About ten minutes afterwards, we heard the announcer say: 'This is The National Broadcasting Service, transmitting in collaboration with sub-stations St. Ann's Bay in the north, Portland Point in the south, Morant Point in the east, and South Negril Point in the west.

'There is still no immediate cause for alarm.

'We are now repeating, in full, the precautions broadcast this morning and earlier this afternoon.

'Inside: remove anything hanging or fixed to walls; store drinking-water; garage all cars, motor-cycles, scooters, and bicycles; put in a stock of lamps, lanterns, candles, kerosene oil, and matches, if absolutely necessary; turn off main supply of electricity, if you care to; collect pots, pans, basins, and other receptacles for protection against possible incoming rain and leaking ceilings.

'Outside: remove fern-pots and veranda furniture; dismantle all clothes-lines, children's swings, hanging pots, and other fixtures; secure zinc-sheeting, boarding-up, and loose shingles and tiles; cut away overhanging tree-branches from walls and roofs; remove all birds and animals to a convenient and safe place; batten down fan-lights, lattice-work, exterior air-conditioning units, doors and windows; and only those people with the appropriate "straight-through" from the front to the back of their houses may leave both front and back doors open or may take them off their hinges, and so divert the high pressure of the wind from the eaves of roofs and from the battened-down doors and windows.

21

'We repeat: there is still no immediate cause for alarm.'
Music.

When we went out to the back-yard, I noticed that there was a slight drop in the temperature. A cool flake of wind was rustling the leaves of the *ackee* and breadfruit trees a short distance away from the work-room.

3

Papa and I got through doing everything in about two hours. Actually I'm ashamed to have to admit it, but he did most of the work; all he wanted me to do was pass him nails and tools and keep out of his way while he was hammering and lifting things about the place.

Naturally, I wanted to do my own fair share. I could have lifted many of the things on my own, but Papa said no. I could have battened down some of the windows and doors, and I could have done the greater part of the bending under the house where Papa wanted to store some lengths of spare piping and zinc-sheeting, but again he objected to my doing the job alone.

Anyway, most of what had to be done was done by Papa. And I had helped here and there, and for the rest, I had watched him enviously.

Afterwards, Mama and Mary brought us sweet-potato pudding and icy cold lemonade made with limes and brown sugar. Papa nibbled at his portion of pudding, took a few sips of his lemonade, and said he was going to lie down and wait for the first signs of the hurricane.

He looked tired and worried. At that moment, I knew that he was thinking about our safety, Mama's, Mary's, and mine. I knew he would blame himself if anything were to happen to us. But Papa must realize that a thing like a hurricane is bigger, in every way, than an ordinary human being?—this I had to ask myself when I'd thought a little more about his tired and worried look. Anyway, even though he didn't seem to know it, I was sure that I could, at least, take care of Mary and myself, if things got very bad later on. As a matter of fact, I was also sure that I could take care of Mama too. Of course, I reminded myself that the old house wasn't all that old, even though it was made of wood and very little concrete. And with the precautions that Papa had taken, hardly any harm could come to us inside.

Mama went back to the kitchen and took Mary with her. Fortunately for Icilda, who helps Mama with the washing, cooking and cleaning, Saturday is her usual day off. At least, she was one person less for Papa to worry about.

Outside began to look very bleak. It was getting cooler as well.

I looked around for something to do, but I could find nothing. I walked about the back-yard and watched the leaves and branches of the trees swaying and dipping much more vigorously than I had noticed when we had all sat down to our snack.

I went inside and looked at the clock on the sideboard. It was saying three forty-five.

I peeped in at the kitchen, but Mama and Mary were not there. They must have gone to lie down too.

I picked up my latest copy of the *Classics Comic,* but after turning a few pages, I put it down and walked over to the radio. Papa had turned it off and I didn't want to disturb him by switching it on again.

Then, quite suddenly, I decided to ring up some of the boys from school. My first conversation was with Four Eyes Dodd.

'Didn't see you at Carib,' I said nice and easy, testing to see what state of nerves old Four Eyes was in at the moment.

'How can you talk about Carib at a time like this, Joe,

23

man?' he said excitedly. 'What about this hurricane business, eh? Noticed anything peculiar?'

'Like what?'

'The strong breeze, man.'

'Cho!'

'Cho, nuh? You wait until it gathers enough speed and blows you straight up to Blue Mountain Peak, boy. You wait!'

'The wind's only background music, Four Eyes,' I teased cautiously. 'I've heard you supply a stronger wind for a film already, man.' I laughed.

He paused and sighed.

'Two different things entirely, Joe.'

'By the way, have you taken precautions yet?'

'Precautions? From early this morning, boy. Not even a hydrogen bomb could touch us, Joe. The whole place is like a fortress, like a real fall-out shelter, if you want to know. D'you remember those pictures we saw in that magazine from the States, the one Moon Face had at the concert at school?'

I said yes.

'Well, that magazine-photographer should see our house now. He should see it from the outside first and then from the inside. Man, he'd want to take at least forty pictures of it and write it up as the safest spot on earth. By the way, you're a "precautions-man" like me—have you noticed how dark it's got?'

'But, Four Eyes, man, it's bound to be dark in your fortress.'

'Not joking, Joe,' he said earnestly, 'I think it's got real dark since one o'clock, you know.'

'So?'

'It's going to get even darker, boy!'

'But I know that, Four Eyes. What colour d'you think *night* is anyway?'

'Not *night,* Joe. I mean in a few minutes' time. Everything is just going to go off *bam*! pure darkness and then *whoosh*!

24

thunder and lightning. Look, Joe, I'll ring you later, eh? I think Daddy wants to use the phone.'

'Later then, Four Eyes.'

'See you, Joe.'

Good old Four Eyes. All he's got for background music now is the wind.

The next person I rang up was Pants Martin. His sister told me that nobody had seen him since he'd gone into the garage to mend a puncture in the front tyre of his bicycle.

When he came to the phone, the first thing he said was: 'Joe, that you? Listen, boy, I'm sorry I couldn't see you at Carib this morning, but the old man wouldn't let me go out at all.'

'That's all right, Pants. I only managed to go by the skin of my teeth. If it wasn't for Mama, I don't think—'

'Joe,' he interrupted me, 'it looks as if this hurricane-warning means business, eh?'

'More or less.'

'More *more* than less, you mean. But tell me something: how many gun-fights this morning?'

'Hurricane-warning? Gun-fights?'

'The film, Joe!'

'Oh, about four, I think.'

'Real good ones?'

'Terrific.'

'Gosh, boy, I wish I had gone.'

'That's all right, Pants. You can out-shoot any of them any time.'

'What about the ending?'

'What about it?'

'Was the show-down shooting nice and loud?'

'Pants, boy, that's when I really missed you.'

'Why?'

'Because you could've shot the Bad Man louder than the Sheriff did.'

'Wish I'd gone, Joe.'

'Never mind. Next week.'

'Yes, next week. Tell me something: d'you think this hurricane might blow down Carib?'

'Never!'

'You can't be too sure, you know, Joe. My old man says that a hurricane is no respecter of concrete and steel.'

'Man, Pants, Carib is like Blue Mountain. Cool and strong.'

'So what's happening to you now?'

'Nothing much. Just waiting.'

'Same here, boy.'

'Ring you later then.'

'Right, Joe.'

Pants, the loudest gunman in the history of Carib—I was glad he was bearing up under the strain.

Of course, if it could actually be done, I'd certainly back Pants to shoot the hurricane right out of existence. One well-placed shot in the dead centre of the 'Eye' of the storm from a 'Pants Special' and that would be the end of the wind, rain, lightning and thunder, for all time.

I rang up Jiji-Wappie Haughton to hear what 'The Great Laughing Man' was thinking of the hurricane situation. As soon as he came on the phone, he gave me a nice big laugh for absolutely no reason at all. Good old Jiji is like that. All the time. At the pictures, in school, everywhere.

So I said to him: 'You won't be laughing like that later on tonight, Jiji.'

And do you know what he said?

'Joe, the whole thing is a Met. Office stunt, man. It's a conspiracy to stop us from going to Carib.'

And he laughed again.

I'm sure Jiji is an incurable laughing jackass.

'So you don't believe the Met. Office, or the *Gleaner,* or the radio?' I was trying to be cautious.

'No, sir!' Jiji sounded very sure of himself, over-confident in fact.

'So, you definitely don't believe there's going to be a hurricane?'

'A little wind and rain, yes. A flash or two of lightning, some thunder here and there, but no big deal like what's expected. People are too easily scared these last days, Joe.'

'So, you haven't taken any precautions at all?'

'Mammie and Daddy have.' He laughed again.

'You must be mad, Jiji,' I said, laughing too.

'You wait and see if I'm not right,' he said seriously. 'Pure false alarm, Joe. Conspiracy, boy.'

'See you, Jiji.'

'See you, Joe.'

I rang up Moon Face Smith but his number was engaged. So was Popeye Mason's and Shaved Head Chin's.

I didn't know what to do next. I thought of ringing up B.B. Perkins, but I honestly, really and truly, couldn't listen to an Arithmetic lesson at all. I mean to say: all that B.B. would want to talk about would be *miles per hour* and that sort of thing.

So, instead of ringing B.B., I went out to the back-yard again and watched the growing wind.

I couldn't help thinking about the speed it would reach later on; perhaps B.B. was right to be so concerned about his *m.p.h.* after all.

I turned round and faced the back of the house. It looked like a big, broad-shouldered man waiting for a firing-squad to come and shoot him down.

Papa had done a marvellous job on the lattice-work round the back veranda. The whole thing had been neatly battened down and two extra push-bolts had been fixed on the door.

I looked up at the roof, and from where I was standing, all the shingles seemed tightly packed and secure. I imagined I saw torrents of rain-water cascading off the roof and the shingles remaining steady as rocks at the bottom of a fast-moving river.

I went back inside. I walked up to Mama's and Papa's bedroom door. I listened and heard Papa gently snoring away. I then walked up to Mary's door and peeped inside. Mary and Mama were asleep on Mary's bed.

I circled back to the dining-room and went up to the radio. I just couldn't touch it.

I went into the sitting-room and sat in front of the other radio which Papa had bought recently to replace the old one on the sideboard in the dining-room, but again, I didn't have the courage to turn it on.

And it was then that I decided to go for a little stroll somewhere or other. Nobody would know. I wouldn't stay away long. I'd be back home before any of them could wake up and miss me—I promised myself.

I felt excited and afraid all at the same time. I knew that Papa would have been angry had he been able to read my thoughts at that precise moment; Mama would have been silent, thinking her own funny thoughts about her disobedient son, the way she always does when I try to pull a fast one on her or on Papa; and as for Mary: I could tell that she would have thought me mad and possibly would have said so quite openly.

I tiptoed out of the house by the back way, crept round the side of the work-room, through the drive-gate, and out into Orange Street. When I got to Torrington Bridge, I turned right and headed for Mary's general hardware store; I have to call it Mary's store because she was the one who had called my attention to it earlier when we heard the first warning being broadcast.

I stood on the piazza by the open double-door and waited for an announcement, just in case there was one coming over

28

in a few minutes' time.

I listened, but all I heard was music, for at least five minutes, together with a few words of explanation from the disc jockey.

When I looked inside, I saw two men battening down the windows at the back of the store and a third climbing a ladder which was leaning against a row of ventilators at the top of the right-hand wall.

Nearly all the stock and the display articles had been covered with tarpaulin.

I listened to the music for a little while longer and then moved on, heading for the Race Course.

4

The Race Course was a prairie all over again. But the grandstand was a dusty mid-West town on its own: an old broken-down Dry Gulch Saloon, an Assayer's Office, a bank, a general store, a barn, an open stable, a blacksmith's shed, a church, a small hotel, and a single row of dwelling houses.

As I walked into town, everybody was talking about the hurricane which was due to blow through at any moment. The Sheriff had had word from the U.S. Marshal, in the neighbouring city, and had warned all the citizens to prepare themselves and their property for sudden disaster.

When I got to the open stable, I saw a few cowhands building a special compartment for the horses and other animals around the town. Cattle were being herded into the church. The pastor had given his permission without raising any objection whatsoever. The Saloon was practically empty. The Assayer's Office and the bank were closed. The general store, in which there was also the post office, was packed with last-minute shoppers, mainly with the women and the old people of the town. The barn had been battened down completely so that the hay, fodder and grain would be protected against the driving downpour of rain.

The entire town was going about its business like an over-crowded ant-hill. I looked around me and all I could see were flashes of black leather shoes scurrying about in the dry dirt of the main street.

All the town had ever had before in the way of natural disasters had been a couple of dust-storms, which hadn't meant a thing as they hadn't lasted very long, and the odd earth tremor. Now it was to get its first tropical hurricane, which had been reported to be travelling at a rate of seventy-five miles an hour all the way from the South Caribbean Area, over Florida, and across to the Middle West.

I went in search of the Sheriff and found him chewing on a dry weed and leaning over the railing outside his office at the jail-house. He nodded and said, 'Howdy, stranger.'

I asked him if I could be of any use to the town, but he shook his head, bit down on the weed, spat, wiped his mouth on the sleeve of his suede waistcoat, and said, 'Nope.'

I figured that the Sheriff, like all the other citizens, must have been too proud to accept outside help. After all, as he had hinted in his greeting earlier, I was only a stranger in town.

I mosied along, looking at everything round me and casually reminding myself that I'd better book in at the hotel at the end of the street before the Big Blow started tearing the place apart.

Just as I was climbing the front steps of the old, wooden, tumbledown hotel, a series of shots rang out behind me. I spun round, my right hand on my Forty-Five, and saw Rango and four other cowboys riding up the main street. So far, they were only shooting up into the air, and I suppose, announcing their evil intentions of taking over the town for themselves.

I wasn't at all surprised that Rango had decided to take

over things at the height of the preparations for the hurricane. It was just the sort of cowardly thing he'd do.

The four cowboys attracted further attention by doing some more shooting, scattered themselves across the street in different directions, and took up strategic positions, while Rango, holding his sawn-off shot-gun level with the Sheriff's face, spoke to him about his intention of seizing the town. The Sheriff was still leaning over the railing outside his office.

In a moment, after the shooting, the entire town had become dead still. All the citizens stood like statues: the men had their arms folded in front of them; the women had their eyes downcast; and the children squatted down beside their parents' legs, looking up, now and then, into their faces to see exactly what they'd have to do if a signal were given to fight against the outlaw cowboys in their midst.

I gazed across at the Sheriff.

Will he continue to be silent and proud?—I wondered. Will he give in to Rango and his men? Will he resist? And if so, how will he arrange it?

The town was waiting for his decision.

In fact, there was very little time left before the hurricane deadline.

Suddenly, giant flashes of lightning began streaking across the mid-West sky. Thunder rolled like a million bass drums. And a gigantic sheet of dust, from the prairie and from the main street itself, came flying in with the speeding wind from the South Caribbean and from Florida, and covered the whole town in less than ten seconds flat: I could see nothing at all; the citizens had disappeared; and so had the four cowboys, Rango, the Sheriff, and the town.

I stared in front of me, and there, appearing as big as life itself, was the grandstand, and spread out around me was the Race Course.

On my way home, I passed Mary's store. It was closed.
There was hardly any traffic crossing over Torrington Bridge.
Orange Street looked desolate and wind-blown.

I kicked an empty cigarette-packet, and helped by the wind,
it went flying up to a mesh-wire fence, through the gap between the strands of wire below the mesh, and into a bed of
ram-goat roses. It settled for a moment and then it took off
again towards the forked trunk of a swaying Bombay mango-
tree.

Somehow, everything seemed just like a mid-West town: the
houses and stores looked stained and parched like early-
morning coffee; the trees were a dusty green; the criss-cross of
the electric and telephone wires above the streets waved like
dark strands in an enormous spider's web; and the streets were
narrow and filled with scraps of fluttering paper and jerkily-
moving tin cans, leaves, twigs, clumps of loose earth, and
other objects. Even the towering, colourful bill-boards seemed
faded and dingy like last year's newspapers.

It was getting steadily darker now. The wind had picked up
considerably and the clouds had a swollen, reddish-grey,
powder-puff look, as if they were trying to droop down towards the earth and spread themselves out.

A plane passed by, droning along like a gravel-throated
bird. I wondered at the time whether it was one of the Met.
Office aircraft or not, but soon I stopped thinking about it,
and with all my might, I began running towards our house
down the street.

Fortunately, when I got home, everybody was still asleep.

Of course, I had had to stay on the back veranda and blow
off steam before going into the house to check. The erratic
way in which I was breathing would certainly have woken up,
not only Mama, Papa, and Mary, but also all our dead

relatives.

I went back to the radio in the dining-room and I grabbed hold of the 'on-off' knob and fought against myself to turn it on. I wanted very badly to know the latest news. I silently accused Papa for sleeping as long as he was; I really did. I even found him guilty of deserting me in the face of the enemy.

In any case, I imagined that, already, certain places in the country parts might very well have had a slight taste of the destruction to come. The southern side of the middle of the Island might possibly be in trouble—why, I did not know; I could not prove it; I was merely guessing and making-believe for my own benefit.

To be honest, I did not even know the general direction of the wind. So, for all I *did not* know, the thing might have been coming straight from Mars or somewhere like that!

So far, I had had no information at all. The radio would be able to give it to me, I knew, but Papa was asleep.

My right hand itched and tingled as it held on to the knob. I gazed at the dial and saw the reflection of my face in it. I made a real frightening monkey-face and laughed quietly after-wards.

I looked at the telephone. I looked back at the radio. I looked across the dining-room into the sitting-room and saw the other radio snugly resting against the wall.

There they were: three things which would be able to give me the necessary information about the progress of the hurricane.

I could use the phone—I remembered. I could ring up the Airport, or Cable and Wireless, or N.B.S., or better still, the Met. Office. Yes, why not?—I asked myself.

I got up and searched for the telephone directory.

Which is it to be?—I wondered.

The Met. Office. Right.

I found the number and was just about to dial it when I

33

heard a voice, behind me, say: 'So you went out, didn't you, Mister Disobedient Joe?'

I turned round and there, rubbing her eyes and yawning, was Mary.

'How did you know?' I asked. 'I thought you were sleeping.'

'Ah!'

She was being *very* cute, and a big nuisance into the bargain.

'Come on, *you*. How did you know?' I insisted.

'Saw you,' she said briefly, annoying me, as she had no doubt intended.

'Saw me? Where?'

'Ah!'

Not again, Mary!—I silently begged her. I felt like holding her and shaking the truth out of her stupid, teasing head.

'All right, Mary,' I said calmly, 'where did you see me?'

'I saw you weren't here.' She yawned again.

Man!—she was being *very, very* intelligent.

'You mean: you missed me?' I said firmly.

'So did Mama and Papa.'

'What!' I was completely ruined. Dead and buried. I realized now that I was done for all time. Papa would really punish me for all he was worth, and Mama would just stand by with that old I-told-you-so look on her face.

'Not to worry,' Mary suddenly said, laughing this time. 'They didn't miss you. I was the only one who did. I got up to get some water from the ice-box and I looked for you everywhere, but couldn't find you. I drank my water and went back to lie down beside Mama. Where were you anyway?'

I told her.

She then sighed the way Mama does in a similar situation, put her head on her left shoulder, and said, 'D'you know something, Joe? The Race Course is going to be your *undoing*.'

She was imitating Mama, and I knew it. But I consoled myself when I remembered that all females, young and old, are

34

pretty much on the same level where tormenting a man is concerned.

I turned my back and picked up the directory, looked at the number again and prepared to dial.

'What are you doing with the phone?' Mary asked.

'Ringing the Met. Office.'

'Why?'

'Why would anyone want to ring the Met. Office on a day like today, Mary? Don't you know why?'

'Why don't you turn on the radio?'

'Papa.'

'You can turn it down low, can't you?'

'I don't want to turn it on at all.'

'Why not, Silly Billy?'

'Not without Papa's permission.'

'You didn't get his permission to go to the Race Course, did you?'

'That was different.'

'How?'

'Because it *was* different.'

'*How*?'

'Don't ask me silly questions, Mary,' I told her, backing out of her third-degree questioning.

Mary's good at that, you know. She reminds me, somehow, of those police officers in the gangster films where the poor suspect is put under a large, bright desk-lamp and cross-questioned for hours on end.

I just wasn't going to stand for Mary's kind of third degree; after all, she was my little sister; and besides, I was the head of the house when Papa wasn't around. I reckoned that when he was sleeping, he was as good as not being around.

So there it was: Mary had to be put in her place.

'What're you going to ask the Met. Office man, Joe?' she asked, changing the subject, as nice as ninepence. She was also very good at doing that, when it suited her.

'Stay and listen, if you want to,' I told her.

I turned round to the phone once more and started to dial the number; then I realized that I hadn't heard the usual dialling-tone. So I stopped, hung up, lifted the receiver again and listened.

The telephone was dead.

PART THREE

EVENING

1

It was now pitch black outside, even though it was only about six o'clock. According to Papa, evening-shadows hadn't had the slightest chance of falling normally because of the unnatural state of affairs. And right after he had said that, I remember Mama swallowing hard and suggesting that instead of saying 'the unnatural state of affairs', why not just say '*your* hurricane'. And then they both laughed.

Outside, the wind was almost howling. I say that because, every now and then, when it blew round the house, it sounded like a series of loud squeals followed by even louder wailing noises, which, when they came together, echoed like the continuous howling of a pack of tormented Alsatian dogs.

By the way, we had all, more or less, got accustomed to the fact that the telephone wasn't working. It had taken us a long time, but finally we did accept the fact. At first, we had all been upset about it: Mary had even cried a little, out of fright, no doubt, at being cut off from the outside world, as she had put it; Mama had nodded thoughtfully and said, 'Well, it looks as if things are really beginning to pop with a vengeance now,' and Papa had said, 'It's probably a little trouble at the telephone company—a loose connexion, perhaps.'

Of course, Papa knew that *we* knew that a loose connexion would have been fixed almost immediately; he must have also known that we had realized that the earlier winds had done a good job, in at least one section of the city already. And, in a way, we'd all known that Papa's so-called 'loose connexion' had been a sample of what was yet to come when the full blast of the hurricane really and truly got going.

The sitting-room radio had been turned on from the time that Papa had got out of bed. We had had about three or four announcements. They had all been fairly similar to one another: they had explained certain simple things about the hurricane: its starting-point somewhere near the Equator, its growing speeds between a hundred-and-twenty miles per hour in a circular shape near the centre and ten-to-fifteen miles per hour in a forward path, its distant location from time to time, and its future direction, which included a part of the eastern section of the Island. The announcements had also said that Key West in Florida would certainly be hit after we had been.

Music was being broadcast at the moment, but, I hoped, not for too long. I wanted to listen to the next announcement, which I knew was going to be the most important and possibly the most terrifying so far. Incidentally, Papa did mention that from the next one onwards, all the announcements were going to take the form of bulletins, which is the proper word to use for very special emergency news broadcasts.

Well, the music was still going on and so was the wind outside.

Quite unexpectedly, Papa spun round in his chair, pointed

38

to Mary and me, and said, 'I think it's time you two were in bed. No arguments either. When the thing actually begins to get moving, it'll be time for all of us to get together in the dining-room, not before.'

I scowled like a two-year-old, as Mama has always described it. But Papa winked at me and said, 'I tell you what: you haven't got to go to bed; just lie down and rest a while, eh?'

I smiled. Mary shrugged.

'I've had my shut-eye, Mary,' Papa said. 'It's only fair that you have yours now.'

I smiled again. Mary pouted.

'If we have to swim for it later,' Papa said, 'we'll need all our strength, Joe, won't we, boy?'

I nodded.

Then Papa added: 'We might even have to put these two on our backs.' He looked at Mama and Mary, and then he chuckled.

Mama looked at me and said, 'If there's any swimming to be done, you two can go straight ahead until you reach the open sea. I'll remain right here. Better the evil you know than the evil you *don't* know.' She slapped her thighs and then folded her arms as if she actually intended to wait for the evil she knew.

Mary got up, stretched, and said, 'I've slept already this afternoon, anyway, and for a long time too. Still, I don't mind going to lie down until the business starts. I'm not going to stay in my room alone, though. I want Joe to come with me.'

Papa looked at me. So did Mama. They had ganged up against me in no uncertain fashion, and they knew it. They were dying to laugh. As soon as we left the room, I distinctly heard muffled sounds of laughter.

Mary turned on the light in her bedroom and closed the door. She sat in her favourite open-back veranda chair which she had had in her room for ages, and I sprawled across her bed.

We said nothing to each other for a few minutes and listened to the wind in the pear-tree just outside the window nearest us. The long, low, whistling sounds came easily through the battening.

We stared at each other but that was all. We would have continued in our silence had not the first, uncertain, sighing downpour of rain caught our attention.

'Rain at last,' I almost shouted. I don't know why I did, but I raised my voice without even knowing it.

'I wish you wouldn't go on as if this thing were a circus or something, Joe,' Mary said, hugging herself against an imaginary gust of cold air, and actually shivering as well.

'This isn't the North Pole, you know,' I began to tease her. 'This isn't—'

'It isn't a merry-go-round in the Race Course either,' she interrupted me angrily.

Then we were silent again. Papa didn't know what he had done for me.

My thoughts wandered a bit: from the boys at school, particularly Jiji-Wappie and B.B., and for two completely different reasons, right on down the line to good old Mother Samuel. My thoughts about the boys led me to believe that Jiji must have realized by now that in spite of himself and his laughter there was going to be a full-scale hurricane and that B.B. must have worked out the whole thing and must have gone on to work out the next hurricane, which mightn't even be due for another ten years or 'next never', as Shaved Head might have said. I thought about Mother Samuel because I imagined that she must have felt that, at least, the first part of her prophecy was coming true: the big deluge. I secretly hoped that the second part would not. The hurricane was here all right, but how could the world think of coming to an end without telling B.B. of all people? Just think of the waste of his great *m.p.h.* calculations if the second part of Mother Samuel's warning were to come true.

My idle thoughts were interrupted by a crashing noise outside. It sounded as though a large tree-branch had been torn off and flung against the side of the house.

There was another crashing noise right afterwards; this time, the flying object, whatever it was it wasn't a tree-branch, slammed itself against the battening across the window.

Then there was yet another crash in the same spot.

Mary got up and headed for the door. I went after her and put my hand on her shoulder. She began to cry softly.

'It's really all right, you know,' I told her, 'it's only the noise that's bad. Whatever it is, it can't hurt us. We're inside, remember?'

She turned round and went back to her open-back veranda chair.

'Let's play,' she said, drying her eyes with the back of her right hand.

'All right,' I said quickly, glad that she had thought of something to take her mind off the frightening sounds of the three crashes. 'Sure, let's play a few rhyming games. What about that one we used to say with Papa?'

'You mean: "*Bright, light; morning, dawning; May, day*"? That one?'

'Yes.'

'No, man, let's play "*I bet I box you . . .*" '

'Right, you begin.'

She got up, walked a little way, stood in the centre of the room, and signalled me over to her.

I went.

Then we began our favourite conversation-game:

Mary: '*I bet I box you.*'

Me: '*You wouldn't venture . . .*'

We laughed. I did so freely, and if the truth be known, mocking myself a little. After all, I knew I was too old for the game. I used to play it when I was about nine or ten, but I had to look after Mary. And as B.B. might have said, 'Politics is politics, man.' I was hoping against hope that Mary hadn't suspected that I was playing with her because I felt that I had to humour her. If there is one thing that she hates it's that. I can't say I blame her eight out of ten times. I hate it too. A lot of older boys are like that, you know. They like to go on as though they're doing you a special favour to talk to you, or play with you, or being around the place when you're there.

Anyway, Mary did laugh a little. Naturally she still sounded nervous and unsure of herself.

'Again?' I asked. We usually did it about three or four times when we were much, much younger.

'All right,' she said. 'You start this time.'

'No,' I objected playfully, 'you start.'

'No,' she said, frowning bad-temperedly and beginning to pout, '*you* start.'

So I did:

Me: '*I bet I box you.*'

Mary: '*You wouldn't venture . . .*'

'Joe! Mary!' Papa called out, rapping at the door. 'The news bulletin's coming over in a few seconds. Come quickly.'

3

We rushed to the door, which Papa had opened for us, and ran straight into the sitting-room.

Mama stared at us and smiled her funny smile.

We sat down and waited.

Then the announcer said: 'This is The National Broadcasting Service, transmitting in collaboration with sub-stations St. Ann's Bay in the north, Portland Point in the south, Morant Point in the east, and South Negril Point in the west.'

'They could have spared us all that business,' Mama complained.

'Station identification,' Papa said. 'The usual thing.'

'N.B.S. hasn't got to identify itself to *me*,' Mama said, having the last word all to herself.

Papa grinned.

'The time is six-thirty precisely.

'We bring you now the latest bulletin on Hurricane Chod supplied by the West Indies' Meteorological Office at Palisadoes.

'Reconnaissance aircraft and shipping reports indicate that, at 5 p.m. Eastern Standard Time, Hurricane Chod was situated at 17.4 degrees north, 75.4 degrees west, or about 115 miles east-south-east of Kingston, and is moving west-north-west at about 15 miles per hour.

'Highest winds are now estimated at 120 miles per hour in squalls within 50 miles of the centre, and winds are gusting to 80 miles per hour already on the eastern tip of the Island. Gales extend out 700 miles in the northern semicircle, 450 miles to the south-east and 225 miles in the south-west quadrant. The lowest central pressure, this afternoon, was 975 millibars or 28.8 inches.'

There was a slight pause, during which Mama said, 'Lord King! I wish there weren't so many figures and point this and point that.'

I thought of B.B. He must have been in his element—what with all those fantastic Maths problems, *m.p.h.*, and things.

'Hurricane Chod is forecast to continue moving west-north-west at 15 miles per hour, and the Eye of the hurricane, which is about 30 miles in diameter, will pass directly over Kingston shortly after midnight. The hurricane-force winds will die down suddenly as the Eye passes over your area but they will increase again suddenly to full force and from the opposite direction as the Eye moves away.

'Stay in safe shelter as the Eye passes over your area. The lull will last from a few minutes up to a maximum of about 1½ hours.'

'He's said "Eye" four times now,' Mary said. 'Four Eyes hurricane!'

Papa frowned and said, 'Shh!'

'Tides will be 2 or 3 feet above normal, and heavy torrential rains will occur, producing flood-threats in low-lying areas. People living in such areas are advised to seek shelter on higher ground. All shipping should stand by for further bulletins.

'All listeners are advised to keep their sets tuned to this frequency for any information which we are able to transmit.'

Papa turned down the volume as the music began again. Even though it was a popular Trinidadian calypso, it sounded out of place. As a matter of fact, it sounded very strange, bright and lively as it was.

All during the bulletin, the wind was raging, and all sorts of things were being flung against the two front doors of the sitting-room. The rain was pelting down in certain spots and cutting across in a forward direction too. The criss-cross was forming a pattern which I hadn't expected to see as I went over to a near-by window and found a tiny space between two lengths of battening. I left that position and put my right eye up to another space on a higher level and saw a shaft of rain moving across the front garden. The rain was travelling just as if it had been thrown, like a cluster of javelins at Championships.

44

'Better go back inside now, Joe,' Papa said, waving his hand towards Mary's bedroom. 'It looks as though we have a very long time to wait.'

'The Eye won't pass until some time after midnight,' Mary said, giving the information in such a way that it sounded as if it were her own and not the Met. Office's, and proving once more that the Eye of the hurricane had, in truth, completely caught her imagination. And why not? It's quite fabulous when you come to think that a thing like a hurricane actually has a shape at all and a centre that resembles an eye, even though it's only a wide circle of calm air and blue sky.

'All right, now, in you get, Miss Mary,' Mama said. Any time she called Mary, Miss Mary, it was a sign that she meant business.

So Mary and I left the sitting-room and went back to the bedroom.

I closed the door and asked, 'D'you want to play some more?'

'What?' Mary asked, pouting a little. She disliked being spoken to like a child, and Mama had just done so, and in front of Papa and me, which was the last thing that Mama should have done really.

'Let's begin with "*I know something . . .*",' I suggested.

'All right, you begin.'

Me: '*I know something.*'

Mary: '*I wouldn't tell a man.*'

Me: '*Corn meal dumpling.*'

Mary: '*Killed a nigger man!*'

'What about "*What you want to be*?" ' she asked, getting into the mood of things.

'Yes, you go first this time.'

Mary: '*What you want to be?*'

Me: '*A Contractor and Builder.*'

'No, you can't be!' she objected. 'Papa's that already.'

'So, why should that stop me from becoming one myself?'

'Because you can't if Papa's one too.'

'But wouldn't you like to be a dressmaker?'

'No.'

'Why?'

'Because Mama's that already.'

'But, Mary, that's no reason—'

'All right, Joe,' she interrupted, 'I'm not playing any more.'

'O.K. I won't be a Contractor and Builder. Begin again.'

She sprawled across the bed and I sat in her chair.

Mary:'*What you want to be*?'

Me: '*President of the United States.*'

'No! No! No! You can't be any such thing,' she objected again.

'Why can't I?'

'Because it's not real.'

'How d'you mean it's not real. A President's real enough. What d'you think the White House is for?'

'Well, you're not old enough.'

'That's all right. I'll grow up.'

'You're not an American, you know.'

'Look, Mary, are we playing a game, or aren't we?'

"Course we are.'

'Well then?'

'All right, I'll start again.'

Mary: '*What you want to be*?'

Me: '*A Sheriff. And you*? . . .'

When she didn't reply, I said the usual '*And you*?' but she said nothing. When I looked at her, I saw, to my surprise, that she was fast asleep. I got up and tiptoed out of the room.

As I was passing through the dining-room on my way to my own room, I glimpsed Papa sitting on the floor and reading the *Gleaner*, and Mama lying on the sofa and darning a pair of my old school socks.

46

How they could be so calm and easy with the wind and the rain raising Cain not more than a few feet away from them, I just didn't know.

I didn't stop.

When I got to my room, I threw myself on the bed without turning on the light. I stared up at the ceiling. I could see very little, really. There was a massive shadow spread out from all four corners, and in it there were tiny flecks of light, bounced on to the ceiling through the fan-light from the bulb in the dining-room.

I raised myself up on my elbows and looked towards the middle window. I searched for the section that had no battens across it; Papa had left a few inches clear at the bottom. I looked at it but I could see nothing through the window-pane; outside seemed even blacker now.

I lay back again.

Suddenly there was a quick, crackling sheet of lightning, followed almost immediately afterwards by a clap of thunder many times louder than a bomb exploding in a war-film. For a second or two, the whole room was ablaze with a light brighter than midday and echoing with a noise greater than any other in the world.

Then there were other flashes of lightning and claps of thunder, cracking away in rapid succession like a sash-cord whip in motion.

I stretched out my arms above my head, felt for my pillow, hugged it, and waited. I wasn't afraid; I was actually thrilled. I felt the way someone feels when he's sitting down in Carib and watching a film that's packed with suspense and big drama.

I began to think of the boys. I was sure that not even Four Eyes would be able to make his famous background music blend in with what was going on outside at the moment. Pants wouldn't be heard even if he'd been mad enough to shoot at the hurricane with all his might. Moon Face definitely wouldn't be heard either even if he'd decided to shout encouraging re-marks at the top of his voice. Popeye, surely, wouldn't think of shadow-boxing with it. Only poor old Shaved Head would cry as he always does. And B.B. would continue to work on the wind, the rain, the lightning, and the thunder, as if they were a giant examination-sum.

I was just about to think of Aunt Maud and how she must have been making out in Westmoreland, when Papa opened the door, and said, 'Another bulletin, Joe. Mary's asleep. You'd better come along, eh?'

As I sat down beside Mama on the sofa, I was just in time to hear the announcer say: 'We have only just received the following progress-reports from amateur radio-, telegraph-, and certain private telephone-messages, coming in from all over Kingston and Saint Andrew. . . .'

While the announcer was talking, I imagined I saw the ex-tent of the damage done to places like the Ward Theatre and the open-air cinemas like the Rialto, the Palace, and the Gaiety. The Ward must have been so badly smashed that I was sure it would look like an old ruin. After all, it's not a modern building, possibly the oldest theatre I've ever seen, and not all that strong enough to stand up to the battering of a hurricane.

The wooden seats in the open-air cinemas must have been soaked through and, for all I knew, wrenched from the con-crete flooring. And all the reels of film and hoardings must have been completely ruined by now.

'Can you imagine what's happened to the Straw Market at Victoria Pier?' Mama said.

'Blown flat, I'd say,' Papa told her. 'Sheds and all.' He shook his head and continued, 'Of course, the thing that's real-ly serious will be the damage done to the Corporation's drink-ing-water reservoirs, and to the light and power stations.'

We listened again to the radio announcer. He was saying:

'. . . and the roofs of a number of dwelling houses have been either partially or wholly blown off. It has been reported that exposed vehicles are being washed away, and in some places damaged by heavy, wind-blown objects. It has also been reported that lightning has struck trees and out-buildings in the City and on estates on the North Coast and on the mid-southern side and eastern tip of the Island. It has been estimated that Kingston has never, within living memory, experienced . . .'

'All the broken telegraph-poles, smashed trees,' Papa was talking again, 'and the flying glass from the wind-shields of parked cars, and that sort of thing.'

I immediately thought about the force of the wind and the lashing of the rain outside. They both sounded extraordinarily louder than ever before, especially after what Papa had just said.

The announcer was saying: 'There are, at present, definite threats of tidal flooding in Morant Bay, Port Royal, Greenwich Farm, Sav-la-mar, Bluefields, and Black River. From a recent telephone conversation with a spokesman from the Met. Office, we have been led to believe that Hurricane Chod will, in fact, have an Island-wide effect. All listeners are advised to keep their sets tuned to this frequency for any further bulletins which we are able to transmit.'

4

Right after listening to the bulletin, we all heard a long-drawn-out creaking sound, a pause, and then a loud, splintering crash.

Papa rushed to the left-hand front window but could not see outside. He crossed over to the right-hand one, bent and looked through a small parting between the lower battens.

Then he turned and said, 'It's the mango-tree. The Number Eleven. Split right across the trunk.'

Mama sighed.

'Anywhere near the house?' she asked afterwards.

'Near enough,' Papa said.

'How near?'

'About a foot or so.'

Just as he'd said that, we heard a slicing, whistling noise which ended in a clattering bang.

Again Papa bent to the parting in the battens and said, 'The drive-gate. The whole thing. Both halves. Right off the hinges.'

'Where?' Mama asked.

'Landed on the veranda steps.'

'Good,' Mama said, 'the next thing to fly will be the house-top. You won't have to bend to see that one, either.'

When Papa left the window, I took my turn. The Number Eleven tree looked like a huge, green, furry monster lying on its side. The slashed stump behind it resembled the gaping mouth of a shark with a mass of jagged white teeth.

And on the front steps, the two halves of the drive-gate lay spread out like the wings of a giant bird of prey.

I also noticed that the evening had got a little lighter out-side. Of course, it was still dark and blurred, but not really as pitch black as it was earlier on.

'Come to me, darling,' I heard Mama say.

When I looked round I saw Mary standing by the sideboard in the dining-room. She was holding the telephone-receiver in her hand.

'What was all the noise about?' she asked. 'It woke me up.'

We told her.

'What are you doing with the phone?' I asked.

'Nothing. Just picked it up without knowing I had, that's all.'

She put the receiver to her ear.

'Dial-tone,' she said, in a matter-of-fact voice. 'It's working again.'

'What did I tell you?' Papa said, smiling broadly and nodding to all of us. 'Must have been a loose connexion at the company.'

Mama sighed again and picked up her darning.

I like the way Mama behaves. It's as though the hurricane is attacking *her* personally. She makes you believe that it's the wind and rain *versus* herself and Papa. At times you'd believe it was really a battle of wits between them and them alone, and that the house was a sort of Madison Square Gardens, and the rest of the population the spectators. As a matter of fact, Mama's attitude makes you feel that the hurricane has nothing to do with you as such. You feel that she has taken everything off your shoulders. You feel that she's prepared to fight and protect you against the terror of the invader. By the way, I've just remembered that phrase from a Mystery Comic I once borrowed from Jiji Wappie.

'I don't suppose you two will want to go back to bed now?' Papa said, looking at Mary and me.

'I don't mind,' Mary said. She sounded like Mama. Cool and strong.

'All right by me, Papa,' I told him.

It was still early in the evening and we had a very long time to wait before the Eye would begin to pass over.

I took the telephone-receiver from Mary and listened to the dialling-tone.

'May I ring up a few of the boys to hear what's happening, Papa?' I asked timidly.

'D'you think they're still up?'

'Maybe.'

'All right. Don't spend all night, though.'

Mary went into the sitting-room and sat beside Mama.

Papa turned down the radio.

As soon as the volume had been reduced, the heavy bombardment of the wind and rain against the front and sides of the house rose suddenly and filled the sitting-room and the dining-room. I felt the house tremble every now and then. The frequent blasts of lightning and thunder had lessened a lot.

Mind you, just before I got Moon Face on the phone, there was a blinding flash and a clanging burst of thunder.

I reminded myself that I must have spoken too soon, even though I hadn't actually spoken out aloud but only thought it.

I asked Moon Face what things were like round his way, and he said, 'Fantastic, man!'

I asked him about the last burst, and he said, 'Just like a rocket smashing the sound barrier, Joe. Just like that, boy.'

'Doesn't need much encouragement from you either, does it, Moon Face?' I said.

He laughed.

He then told me how badly his house was leaking, how new it was, and how anxious and worried his parents were. They lived in Mona Heights.

'Can you swim, Moon Face?' I teased.

'Like lead,' he said.

'Got an inner tube?' I teased again.

'Not even an elastic band.' He pretended to be upset about the fact.

'But you're a great shouter, Moon Face, man. You can always shout for help.'

'Might lose the voice, Joe.'

We laughed and rang off.

I phoned Popeye next. He was really worried.

'It's my guinea-pigs, Joe,' he explained. 'They're soaking wet, boy. I left them in the out-room and the roof is nearly off. Mother won't allow me to rescue them at all.'

'How far have you got to go?' I asked out of sympathy.

'Just a few feet from the back veranda.'

'Can't you give her the slip?'

'Eyes in the back of her head, Joe.'

'So, no hope, eh?'

'Never!'

'Why?'

'Can't twist. Everybody's watching like hawks circling round me, boy.'

'Think they'll drown, Popeye?'

'Guinea-pigs are so funny. I don't know.'

'Can they swim?'

'Don't know.'

'What're you going to do then?'

'Don't know.'

Popeye and I talked a little longer about the general state of things and I told him not to worry too much about his guinea-pigs, but he sounded very hopeless to me. I promised to look out for a new pair for him if his drowned. He said he'd never keep any more if anything happened to the ones he had now. I couldn't blame him. I told him I was sorry and said good-bye until after the hurricane.

I tried to get Shaved Head but his phone rang and rang. I tried again. Nothing.

Papa looked at me, and I knew exactly what he meant. I hung up and went back to my room. Just as I was taking off my shoes, Mary came in and sat on the bed.

'Want to play some more?' she asked.

'I don't think Papa would like that,' I told her, grinning a little to soften the blow.

'Doesn't matter,' she said.

'Explain.'

'Well, Papa and Mama are far away. Can't you see they're worried?'

I honestly hadn't noticed that they were far away, according to Mary, and I didn't think that Mama was worried, either. Anyway, I didn't want to start an argument, so I said, 'What's it to be this time?'

'Anything,' she said carelessly, flouncing and throwing up her hands and letting them drop with a padded *plop* on her skirt.

'Rhymes?' I asked.

'All right.'

I began:

Me: '*. . . man on the flying trapeze.*'

Mary: '*Mama's Sunday rice-and-peas.*'

I hesitated, thought a bit, and decided it was hopeless. I couldn't go on. She looked at me. I avoided her stare.

'That wasn't such a good one,' she complained. 'What about *Little Sally Water?*'

That one was child's play, real infants' play in fact; and not only that, it was little girls' play. I decided not to answer her.

'All right then, you suggest something else,' she said, *plopping* her hands on her skirt in rapid succession, as if to warn me that she was due to explode any second.

Of course, I didn't know what to say. I didn't want to hurt her feelings. I knew that she was depending on me to keep her company, to amuse her, to share whatever we had to share between us. I knew that the horrible noises outside were making her uneasy; they were also enough to make even *me* feel slightly uncomfortable.

The point is: I could have dealt with the situation had it been one of the boys facing me. I could have come up with something which would have satisfied both parties.

But how was I to bob and weave with a girl?—and my own sister at that! She just wouldn't be able to cope with all the tactics, all the twists and turns, all the rough stuff, and so on.

I mean to say: had it been Four Eyes, we could have done a bit of wrestling or gunplay or something like that.

So I said, 'Let's ask Papa if we can listen to the music for a few minutes. Afterwards we might feel like sleeping for a while. O.K.?'

When poor Papa saw us approaching him, he smiled.

'Thought as much,' he said. 'No rest for the wicked.'

We sat on the floor beside him and listened to the hurricane and to the radio; at least, I know I did, and I imagine Mary did too.

'I think I'd better start looking for leaks,' Mama said, getting up and throwing my socks at me.

They were neatly darned. I thanked her.

When she came back, she said, 'Two big leaks in our bedroom, one in the kitchen, one in your bedroom, Mary, and about three or four in the bathroom. The place seems to be more *holey* than *righteous*!'

Mary and I giggled.

'So, in here, the dining-room, the corridor, and Joe's room are all right?' Papa asked.

'For the time being,' Mama said, 'until the roof decides to fly away like Peter and Paul.'

We giggled again.

'Looks to me,' Mama continued, 'as if the whole house would like to pack up and take a holiday or something.'

'It isn't a new house, you know,' Papa said.

'You can go on defending it,' Mama said. 'I know that Noah's Ark, after all these centuries of bouncing up and down on top of Mount Ararat and floating all over the world and resting somewhere after that only God knows where, just couldn't be in a worse condition than this house.'

And it was then that we all heard it. At first, it began with a slow, high-pitched screeching sound; then it became a steady, deep, tearing noise as if someone were ripping a sheet of awning-cloth; and, in a short time, it sounded like a giant nail being wrenched out of a piece of hard wood by a giant hammer-claw.

We looked at one another.

'It's the work-room,' Papa said calmly. 'The roof.'

We listened.

The pressure of the wind began whistling through the gap and the wrenching, straining, scraping sounds continued.

Then they stopped.

'The wind's changed direction,' Papa said.

'Will it change back again?' Mary asked.

'It might.'

'Soon?'

'Perhaps.'

The thing that made me scared at that moment was our helplessness. Whatever the wind wanted to do we had to stay inside and let it do it. Yet, I wasn't scared for long. Without being able to explain it to myself, for the first time that day I really felt fighting mad. If I could have shouted at the wind, or battered it with my fists, or punched it flying, I certainly would have done so.

Then it happened.

There was a loud groan, a screeching lift and a dip, another screeching lift, another groan, and then *whoosh*!—the work-room roof was off.

5

Mama got up and said, 'What about the equipment?'

Papa said, 'Everything's covered over, more or less. One or two things might get soaked, but the bulk of the machines and so on ought to be all right.'

Mama left us. She said briefly, before she slipped out of sight, that she was going to the kitchen to get a few pots and pans to put under the leaking ceilings in the rooms she'd mentioned earlier.

Mary went with her.

Papa and I stared at each other.

'At least,' he said, 'we've still got electricity and the telephone's working.'

'Yes,' I said, 'until the wind knocks them out completely.'

'Might not, you know,' he said, 'we might just be that little bit lucky.'

'We'll need plenty of luck, Papa,' I said, clenching my fists and remembering the thought I had had about knocking the wind for six.

Then we were silent again.

I suppose we were both listening to the roaring downpour of rain and the lashing of the wind, and hoping against hope that the body of the house itself wouldn't be seriously damaged. I thought about the house that Papa was planning to move to. It was somewhere in the back of my mind that terrible things were, at that very moment, happening to it, too. After all, it was in Harbour View. And the announcer had said that many houses in Mona Heights, Harbour View, and Port Royal were being badly affected by high winds and flooding.

Anyway, I secretly hoped that Tuna Avenue would be spared, if only for Mama's sake.

I knew that Papa must have been thinking about the equipment in his work-room. I felt really and truly sorry for him.

He just sat there, his head bent, his hands folded across his chest, and stared into space.

The sweet music of *Linstead Market* was coming from the radio. I like that *mento* very much. I know Mama does too. She usually hums it, especially while she's working at her sewing-machine.

' "Wat a Satiday nite" is right,' Papa said, and he started to sing the rest of the chorus off-key.

A few minutes passed and Mary and Mama came back, one before the other, to the sitting-room. I wondered why Mary had come in before Mama, but when I looked I saw Mama

57

buttoning up the back of Mary's dress.

Mary is always so slow that I'm accustomed to seeing her come into a room seconds after anyone else she may have been walking with.

The *mento* had finished and *Stormy Weather* was being played.

Mama said, 'Somebody up at N.B.S. has a real ripe sense of humour, playing a song like that at a time like this.'

Papa smiled.

I sniggered politely.

Mary just looked at us askance and said nothing one way or another.

'Well, what about a second bold try, you two?' Mama asked. 'No use your waiting up any longer. Your father will wake you when the famous Eye is passing over.'

'Yes,' Papa backed her up. 'Definitely.'

Mary and I nodded, as we were expected to whenever 'Mama-pressure' took us. I was quite accustomed to it. If Mama turned on the pressure and you were in the way, there was no side-stepping it at all. Papa wasn't too bad. He turned on his own brand of 'Papa-pressure' only now and then.

'Right,' Mama reminded us, 'straight to bed, both of you. No dilly-dallying.'

'Try the phone again, Joe,' Papa said.

Mama frowned.

I got up and took Mary's hand, and we walked across to the dining-room.

I lifted the receiver.

The dialling-tone had gone again.

I told Papa so, and he said, 'Thought it might have. The roof must have sliced the wires.'

Then suddenly Mary broke down and cried.

Mama tried to comfort her by telling her that we would all keep her company and that we weren't really cut off from the outside world at all. But after Mary had sobbed for a while, she stopped abruptly, leant forwards, hung her head, and screamed.

I honestly thought her heart would break.

And it was at that precise moment that there was a deafening series of crashes outside, and all the lights went out.

6

Mama held on to Mary and me, and Papa bent to the right-hand window and looked through the parting between the battens.

'The front garden's the same,' he said, half muttering to himself and half talking to us. He sounded like a man in a trance. 'The Number Eleven's still on its side. The drive-gate's on the steps. Nothing else has fallen, as far as I can see.'

'You're not looking far enough,' Mama said urgently.

'Still can't see anything different,' Papa said.

'I don't believe in ghosts,' Mama said. 'You look again.'

Papa said, 'The place is the same.'

'I distinctly heard what you and the children heard,' Mama insisted. 'Something must have happened out there.'

'No. Nothing.'

'Look towards the street, if you can see that far.'

Papa was silent for a few seconds. We waited in silence too.

Strangely enough, Mary had stopped screaming, and Mama was breathing hard.

'Lord!' Papa cried out.

'What?' Mama asked.

'The electric-cables. They're dangling all over the place. I can see at least three poles on the ground and another broken in half.'

'We'd better disconnect our main-switch inside, don't you

think?' Mama asked.

'It's been done for us already from outside,' Papa said, shaking his head from side to side and chuckling to himself.

'You never mind that,' Mama said. 'Disconnect the thing all the same.'

Papa straightened up, nodded, went across to the corridor to the fuse-box, and did so.

No radio, no telephone, and no light—*bangarangs,* as Four Eyes would have said, had begun—the blackout was now complete.

PART FOUR

MIDNIGHT

1

I took a long time to drop off to sleep. I kept tossing and turning and thinking about the darkness in the whole of the house. The shadowy, inky gloom of my own room didn't matter very much, but the sudden blacking out of the sitting-room and the dining-room kept coming back to me time and again. In fact, it haunted me.

So did the hurricane.

And finally, with both those buzzing and banging around in my head, I fell asleep.

2

Papa woke me at about five minutes past midnight. He told me that I'd been sleeping nearly five hours. He also said that

Mary was still asleep and that he'd decided not to wake her.

We walked into the sitting-room to join Mama, who was lying on the sofa.

Then he said, 'The Eye, Joe. It's passing over now.'

It was only after he'd said so that I noticed how quiet everything had become.

It was dead still, like a cemetery at night, like Ward Theatre during the day, like a classroom during holiday-time.

It was also very hot and stuffy. There was a kind of steam-heat settling in the air, rising up into my nose, and getting into my throat; I suppose I imagined it, but it was too much like being suffocated for it to have been completely in my imagination.

It was just like it was before the winds had started in the late afternoon.

My hands felt clammy. They felt the same way they had when Mary and I had gone walking in the Race Course after breakfast.

My forehead was damp with perspiration and my head felt light and reavy all at the same time.

I noticed that Mama had found her ancient box of candles and had set two on the dining-table, two more on the radio in the sitting-room, and one next to her elbow on the side-table by the sofa. They were burning jerkily; and bright though they were, they weren't exactly bright enough to break up all the darkness in the two rooms.

Mama had the family Bible open on her lap. I said to myself, 'I bet she's been reading good old Psalm 91.'

I peeped and saw that I was right.

'What're you looking at?' she asked.

'Psalm 91, Mama?' I said.

'Yes, son. It's always a comforter. And apart from that, the words are lovely to read. I only wish you'd read the Bible the way you devour those comics of yours.'

62

I knew that was coming.

So I said, 'We read a lot of Scripture at school, you know, five times a week, sometimes more.'

'School-reading and reading for consolation and pleasure are two horses of a different colour,' she told me, quite seriously.

Just to annoy her, I said, 'But the Bible isn't a horse, Mama.'

'A manner of speaking, Joe,' she said. 'Just a manner of speaking.'

Papa laughed when I made the remark about the Bible not being a horse and she had said to him: 'Don't you encourage him in his evil ways now. Like father, like son.'

'Gosh, boy,' I said to Papa, hoping to change the subject, 'it's really quiet, eh!'

He nodded.

'It's a funny thing, but you get this same sort of silence when there's a drought on, you know, Joe,' he said.

'Really?' I felt a story coming up from his big collection of old-time stories about the bad days when he was a child in the country.

Incidentally, I love it when Papa tells those stories. He's a marvellous story-teller, really.

'You see, Joe,' he began, 'long before you were born, before you were even thought of—as a matter of fact, it was 1933—there was a very, very bad drought on the land, about seventeen months of it, to be exact. It began in April 1932.'

'Lord!' Mama interrupted. 'Spare us another like that one. I remember it only too well.'

Papa nodded.

He said, 'Well, Joe, the drought, as you know, is a dry time—no rain, no moisture for the ground, no nourishment for crops or anything. Things were very hard for everybody, for those in the country-parts, those in the towns, and for those in Kingston.'

63

'Things were thin, *very* thin to say the least,' Mama agreed. 'The entire population suffered—bottom, middle and top.'

Papa continued: 'I used to pass by and see fruit trees and other plants withering away, day by day. I used to see river-beds drying up. Dust was everywhere. Flies were everywhere. And then there was this silence over everything. It was as though there had been a blanket thrown right over the land . . .'

Just at that point in Papa's story, my mind started to wander a bit. I would not have allowed myself to do that ordinarily, but I was dying to know what was going on outside. Suddenly I felt caged in, almost on the verge of suffocation. Listening to Papa's voice actually made my sense of imprisonment quite unbearable. There I was, locked in, battened down like a window, and the Eye was passing over. I wanted to break down the front door and rush outside. I wanted to run out to the street and stand and stare the Eye in the face and see it for myself. I was certain that I would have been the only one of the boys who would have done so. I thought how they'd all envy me when they could do nothing but sit and listen to me describing the size of the Eye, the way it hung over me, how it moved, and how I stood alone and out-stared it.

'. . . and on *that* weekend,' Papa was saying, 'the highest rainfall, in any one spot on earth, was recorded in Portland: one hundred and seventeen inches of rain fell in about eight hours.'

'And the drought was no more,' I said, just to cover up in case Papa had noticed that I had not been listening, and also to conceal my regret for not having paid attention to what must have been a very interesting story.

'Yes, son, and the drought was no more,' Papa said, shaking his head from side to side at the wonder of it all.

'What would be a very nice thing,' Mama said, 'is if we could say the same about this hurricane right now.'

Papa laughed. So did I.

And Papa said afterwards: 'Life's like that. You either get too much of a thing, or not enough of it.'

We were certainly getting a lot of calm now. I began to look around at the candles. Their thin little lights looked gentle and old-fashioned. It's very funny when you come to think of it, but their small shimmering flames made the place look like an old house in the country, like Aunt Maud's place, even though she used oil-lamps with wide, white lampshades.

3

A little while afterwards, Mama got up, brushed some imaginary crumbs from the front of her dress as she always does, stretched and yawned, and said that she was going out to the kitchen to prepare us something to eat. In a way, I was glad she was leaving us alone. I wanted to ask Papa's permission to take a look round outside, and I knew, with Mama still in the room, he would have been compelled to say no.

As soon as she had left, I said casually, 'It's going to be calm like this for quite a while, isn't it, Papa?'

'Well, the radio said anywhere from a few minutes up to an hour and a half, I think,' he told me. 'Why?'

I knew he had suspected my reason for asking.

'We could take a peep outside,' I suggested.

'I suppose we could.'

'Let's,' I said, glad that he hadn't objected.

He didn't answer me right away. He hesitated, looked down at his hands, fanned out his fingers, and shook his head thoughtfully.

'What about it, Papa?' I asked, perhaps a trifle too impatiently.

He didn't reply.

We sat in silence for a few minutes, maybe two minutes in

all.

I tried again.

'Of course, you know, Joe,' he said finally, 'we might just as well wait until the whole thing's over later on in the morning.'

'But,' I said urgently, 'it might go on and on for hours and hours once it starts up again.'

All Papa said to that was, 'Humm.'

I knew I was losing the argument.

I wondered how best to tackle the situation again. I had to have another try before Mama got back with our snack.

'We could stand in the corridor and look out through the side door across the veranda. You didn't batten down that door, Papa, did you?'

'No, I didn't, son.'

'Well?'

'But, couldn't we wait, Joe?'

'It's calm *now*, Papa!'

'Suppose we're caught by surprise?'

'We can always close the door quickly and duck back inside in a flash.'

'Suppose Mama catches us, eh?'

Ah! so *that* was it. Why hadn't I guessed?

'So you're not afraid of the wind then?' I asked bluntly.

'Oh, yes, that too.' He laughed. 'No, Joe, we'd better wait until later.'

Just as he had said that, Mama came back in with a tray of double-decker bully-beef sandwiches bulging with salad tomatoes, lettuce, and dripping slightly with mayonnaise, and three large cups of steaming hot country chocolate.

She said, 'I heard you, you know, Mister Joe.'

'What, Mama?' I asked nervously, knowing full well that she must've been listening all the while.

'Want to look outside, do you?' she said, teasing me as only she knows how. 'What is all this about, eh? What if something falls and clouts you on your head? You can never tell what the wind and the rain haven't loosened on the roof and elsewhere, you know.'

'What's to fall must've fallen already, Mama,' I pleaded.

'You know something, Joe? You really don't know when you're well off, my son. Can you imagine how many poor unfortunate people are, at this very moment, without a roof over their heads? Can you?'

'A few, I suppose.'

'A *few*? Well, let me tell you: for your information, there must be hundreds all over the countryside, and about the same amount in and around Kingston.'

'So, we don't look outside then?' I asked, putting the finishing-touch to my hopeless question which I had asked Papa earlier.

Papa shook his head.

Mama sighed heavily. And it was a sure sign that our little talk was over for all time.

I bit into a sandwich and realized for the first time just how ravenously hungry I was. I *wolfed* down two more in quick succession, as Mama would have said had she been watching me, and sipped the hot chocolate slowly. Somehow I imagined that eating in a jet-plane at top speed would have given me the same sensation as I was now feeling. The caged silence was the thing that made me think so, and of course, also the way in which Mama, Papa, and I were sitting together in a straight line on the sofa.

In less than no time at all, I was imagining all sorts of make-believe dreams about all sorts of people, things, and happenings.

And, naturally, without knowing it, I fell asleep.

4

My dreams were, I still remember, very erratic at first. I caught glimpses of the front part of our house, the back-yard, and the roofless work-room; then I saw the grandstand in the Race Course and the main entrance to Wolmer's Boys' School.

Mixed up with these snap-shots of dreams, I saw Mother Samuel standing on a milk-box in front of Mary's hardware store, B.B. painting a number of plus- and minus-signs on a tall bill-board at Torrington Bridge, Four Eyes sitting on the bridge and conducting a fantastically big orchestra of monkeys and chimpanzees, Pants shooting cannon-balls in the eye of the Eye of the hurricane, Jiji-Wappie laughing at Pants, Moon Face encouraging Pants, Popeye applying a *full-nelson* on the Eye, and Shaved Head sobbing his heart out at the bottom of the front steps at Carib because the film he'd just seen had been a comedy.

Then my erratic dreams stopped.

Right after that I saw Mama sewing an enormous flag of some unknown country, and Papa supervising the building of a beautiful modern house on Tuna Avenue in Harbour View.

These two dreams lasted the longest of all those I had had.

The one with Mama in it was ordinary and everyday. She just kept on sewing and the flag kept on spreading itself all over the machine, over Mama's lap, on the floor, and almost out to the corridor.

The other, with Papa in it, was extraordinary and a little bit mysterious.

You see: the house he was building began disappearing from time to time and then re-appearing right afterwards. It came and went, back and forth, until it looked like the shimmering reflection of a house in the mirror of a pool of water which is being disturbed by a gentle breeze.

And so it went on.

68

PART FIVE

NEXT MORNING

1

When I awoke, the hurricane was blasting away again, like a jet-plane warming up in a locked hangar. Every now and then there were other violent stabbing blasts, like a batch of pneumatic drills boring away in an enclosed hill-side quarry. I couldn't believe my ears for the noise in the sitting-room. It was even more booming than the first part of the hurricane had been; it was faster too.

I asked Papa what time it was, and he said it was almost three o'clock. Then he said that the Eye had lasted a little longer than had been expected; it had continued for more than two hours.

Both he and Mama began to tease me for being dead to the world for so long a time. They said that I had done all sorts of funny things in my sleep: I had squirmed, twitched, talked, giggled, and laughed out loud.

'At one stage of the game,' Papa said, 'we were going to wake you, Joe. We thought you were going to kill yourself laughing.'

That must have been during the first part of my erratic dreams, I said to myself, possibly when I was looking at the boys carrying on at Torrington Bridge.

'No wonder, Joe,' Mama said, 'all those sandwiches—goodness! You *wolfed* them down like a hound who hadn't seen food for weeks.'

I wanted to tell them about the flag of the unknown country and the beautiful house that kept disappearing, but I changed my mind; I knew they would have laughed at me.

So, instead, I asked about the hurricane.

'It's blowing from the opposite direction now, son,' Papa said. 'It usually does after the Eye has passed.'

Mama sighed and said, 'If it didn't catch you going, it certainly catches you coming back.'

Then Papa added, 'As a matter of fact, what it does is this: on its first go, it bends all the toughest things one way, and on its second go, it finishes off the job by breaking them with an even stronger wind blowing from the opposite side.'

'Were there any more crashes when I was sleeping?' I asked.

'A few,' Papa said.

'Near the house?'

'Some of them.'

'Is the main roof all right?'

'Hope so. At least for your mother's sake; she's not such a good swimmer, you know.' Papa chuckled.

'How fast d'you think the wind is now?' I asked.

'Oh, a hundred-and-twenty,' he said casually, 'maybe more.'

Mama yawned.

'I hope Mary's all right,' she said, taking no notice of Papa and me and of our conversation.

Then she got up and went to see if Mary was covered up

and sleeping soundly.

Now that I was alone with Papa, I decided to ask, 'It will be, more or less, all right if we go out together after it's finished, won't it?'

'We can walk around a bit, yes,' he said, rubbing his eyes and stifling a yawn. 'Where would you like to go?'

'I think I'd like to go round to Shaved Head's place, and maybe, look for the rest of the boys afterwards.'

'That's a lot of walking, son,' he said, smiling as he always does whenever I say something quite impossible or unreasonable.

'Well, we can walk around the area for a start anyway,' I suggested more reasonably, I thought.

'Fine by me,' Papa said, yawning again.

In the middle of his yawn, there was a splintering crash outside. For a moment, I had the silly idea that it had all happened in Papa's yawn, in the way that terrible sounds are sometimes heard to come from the open mouths of certain animals and people in Walt Disney cartoon films. It seemed just like that, really.

'Another tree,' Papa said, taking it easy, as if it had been the hundredth tree that had crashed round the house.

The awful splintering crash was repeated soon afterwards.

Papa said, 'And another.'

Mama came in and sat between us: 'I'm glad Mary's sleeping through it. By the way, what was the last one?'

'Two since you left,' Papa told her, 'both trees, I think.'

'So, the old house seems to be shaping all right, eh?' Mama said. 'I really had visions of the roof flying across the Race Course by now.'

Then we were silent.

In a way, I suppose we were waiting for the house itself to be uprooted by the wind. I don't think any of us could have been actually wishing it to happen, but we were certainly expecting it.

Then we heard a shower of shattering glass, followed by another shower, and yet another.

'The windows in the front bedroom,' Mama said.

'Sounded like the side ones to me,' Papa said.

'Might very well be,' Mama agreed, 'if the thing's blowing from the other end now.'

'The battens must have been torn off first,' I suggested.

We were silent again.

We waited.

Nothing. Only the raging wind.

All of a sudden the house began to tremble all over. Perhaps a better way of saying it would be: it began to shudder. It shuddered for a while in the way someone does when he gets goose-pimples all over his flesh, either from fright or from a change of hot to cool air.

We looked at one another and I saw Mama reaching out for the Bible.

Papa got up and started walking about.

The shuddering movement stopped abruptly.

Then, in a matter of seconds, it began again. This time it was longer and more powerful.

Mama began to read Psalm 91 aloud, even though she knew the whole thing by heart.

Papa continued to walk up and down the sitting-room, stopping now and then to test the floor-boards with his weight, or pat the back of a chair, or put either of his feet on the cross-pin at the back of the upright—a habit of his, I knew, Mama did not like at all. But she was much too busy with her reading to notice him.

She was saying:

'A thousand shall fall at thy side,
And ten thousand at thy right hand;

But it shall not come nigh thee.
Only with thine eyes shalt thou behold—'

After a while, there was yet another shuddering sensation. It was the most powerful so far. Yet, it was the shortest.

As soon as it had passed, we heard a low, rumbling sound, followed by a louder rolling one, followed by another rumble, and yet another thunderous roll, and then, finally, a caving-in murmur and a roaring crash.

Mama and I jumped up at the same time. Papa ran ahead of us out of the room and into the corridor. When we got there, he had disappeared. We followed after him and looked in at the front bedroom; he wasn't there, and the room was all right. After that, we looked in at Mary's room; that was all right. We turned sharp left into the kitchen; and that was all right.

Then we heard Papa's voice. 'Don't come any farther!' it said. 'It's the bathroom wall. More than half of it. Torn away.'

The words came in loud spurts, bobbing up and down and swaying about on the surging wind which had, by now, got partly inside the house because of the gap in the wall.

But, as soon as Papa and I had managed to close the door of the bathroom, the pressure became less, and so did the surging noises. Of course, the usual roaring continued outside.

When we got back to the sitting-room, we saw Mary sitting on a chair at the side of the sofa. She looked sleepy-eyed and scared. Mama hugged her and soothed her.

Papa and I talked quietly about the damage.

'I'll have to batten down the door from the outside,' he said, tapping his chin lightly with the thumb and forefinger of his right hand. 'The wind's bound to smash it in towards the corridor in no time at all.'

'Would you like me to help you?' I asked.

'All right, son,' he smiled. 'As you're a good swimmer, I'll

73

take the risk.'

Papa and I moved briskly about the house, testing all the windows and doors as we went along. Our first big job was seeing to the bathroom door, which we had to repair as quickly as we could. We roped the knob and metal handle to two other doorknobs on the same side of the corridor and nailed down the hinges and also the part of the door that closed on to the floor of the corridor.

Of course, when we were working on the door, I stared through the gap in the bathroom wall and got a good look at the hurricane as it blasted its way down the side-yard. The speed of the wind sounded as though it were being jet-propelled, and the rain, that travelled with it, tore into us like bullets.

Papa looked at me once or twice and I got out of range to please him.

After that, we worked on a number of leaks with the plasterers' putty which Papa had entrusted to me to mix for the very first time ever.

Just as we had finished, I heard Mama cry out. Papa had not heard. He was busy testing the battens across the door of the ironing-room. I told him about Mama, and we hurried off to her.

She was hugging Mary.

'Look,' she said, pointing to the front part of the sitting-room floor.

Water was flooding in under the three doors which opened on to the front veranda.

Papa said coolly, 'So that means that the water has risen higher than the veranda.'

' 'Course it has,' Mama said, almost bad-temperedly. 'How else could it have reached as far as the sitting-room?—You tell me that.'

But what looked like a tough spot for Papa was soon by-passed because of something that happened quite quickly and unexpectedly.

2

And this was it: a split second after Mama had said what she had to Papa, the ceiling of the sitting-room began to leak right above her head; the first few drops of water hit her flush on her nose and spilled on to Mary's cheek.

Mary was the first to laugh. I followed. And then Mama herself broke down. Shortly afterwards, Papa collapsed on the sofa and roared.

It was a good thing that that had happened at the time it had, because, somehow, all four of us had been on edge and we might have started being most unpleasant to one another had we gone on and on.

Needless to say, we were all nervous about the water flooding into the house. I, for one, began feeling a creeping sense of panic rising to my throat. I was again getting that sensation of being trapped, and this time by unseen water, as it were. I looked up at the ceiling and down once more to the floor, and I shuddered slightly at the thought of the sitting-room becoming a pool of water. Papa and I would be all right, but what about Mama and Mary, I wondered. I thought, too, about the possibility of trying to escape. How? Where to? And what about the things, all our personal property, we would lose or have to leave behind if we did manage to escape— Mama's, Papa's, Mary's, and my own?

I'm sure the others were thinking the same. I watched Mama's face and Mary's. They were tired and strained. I looked across at Papa but he wasn't there. During my reverie, he had dashed off to the back of the house and I could hear him rummaging about. In next to no time, he brought back several rolls of canvas sheeting and lots of other stuff to take care of the flooding. Then he and I got down to work.

3

At about five o'clock in the morning the rain suddenly stopped and the wind died down slowly and gracefully like an enormous box-kite lowering itself out of the sky and fluttering its way down on the grass a few yards away from your feet.

The calm, that the dead hurricane had left behind, was perhaps even more haunting than the one that the Eye had brought earlier at midnight.

I really can't say how the others felt, but I know that I felt suddenly peaceful and completely empty inside. If the truth be known, I felt absolutely drained and tired, as if a great load had been lifted off my back. In a way, I suppose, I felt as if the hurricane had subsided at my feet and I had been left standing over it, just as though I had fought against it and beaten it into the ground.

I may have been imagining it, in fact I am now sure I must have, but then I sensed a tingling in the air, the sort of feeling you end up by getting after a very cold shower first thing in the morning. The tingling wasn't only in me; it was all around me in the room.

That plus the calm added up to a sensation of magic and mystery.

Mary was sleeping with her head on Mama's lap, and Mama was nodding and dozing off when it happened. Papa and I were quiet all along, thinking our separate thoughts, and no doubt, refusing to drop off to sleep.

Now that we had seen the end of the hurricane for ourselves, we merely looked at each other and said nothing. It had been all too sudden for us really.

A few seconds passed, then Papa said, 'Well, that seems to

be that, Joe. Unless, of course, the thing has more than one Eye.' He chuckled quietly.

'No, Papa,' I whispered so as not to wake Mary or disturb Mama, 'this must be the end of it. There couldn't be more to come.'

And there wasn't.

4

At about nine o'clock, after we had all slept off the worry and anxiety of the hurricane, Papa and I announced to Mama and Mary that we intended doing two things: first, we were going to clear up the place outside as best we could and help straighten up the inside of the house, and second, we were going to take a short walk to see the extent of the damage along Orange Street, Slipe Road, and at Cross Roads.

Mama fixed us a fabulous Sunday morning breakfast of *ackee,* salt fish, tiny cubes of fried fat pork, pear, hard dough bread, and country chocolate. It's true that we had had a similar breakfast the morning before, but somehow that didn't matter. In any case, *ackee* and salt fish has always been a Sunday morning meal in our house.

And the funny thing is: had you seen the way we devoured everything, you would have said that, for once, we were really all wolves.

Afterwards, Papa and I took down the battens, mopped up the floor-boards, plugged the leaking spots in the ceiling with putty, did a few small repair jobs here and there, and set about clearing up the back- and side-yards and the front garden.

Of course, we had gone ahead and attempted this even though the flood water had not begun to subside nearly enough to allow us to do the jobs we had wanted to do outside. But we did our best, hopefully splashing about with what must have seemed a mixture of defiance and playful recklessness. In fact, we did very little work. However, we lifted the drive-gate and dropped it back on its swing-free hinges, and we banked a few cumbersome twigs and branches on the topmost ridge of the rockery round the Number Eleven mango-tree, which the hurricane had snapped in two.

Naturally, Papa was very unhappy about the damage done to his work-room. We spent a long time drying things and wiping the metal parts of the many tools, instruments and pieces of equipment that got drenched in the rain-water. At the end of it, we both realized that it was going to take a whole month or more to put everything right again and even longer to rebuild the roof.

Papa gave me a long, sad look, and he must have seen how I felt about the whole unfortunate business, because he winked at me and said, 'Big men don't cry, Joe. They plan.' And he gripped my shoulder, winked again, and we left the work-room together.

Somehow I was sure that from then on Papa and I would be very much closer to each other. We had become partners and co-planners.

5

Having done all that, we left Mama and Mary to their housework and went for our walk up Orange Street.

Everything was dead calm. The sky was a deep blue, and the clouds were very, very high, almost near vanishing-point. No one would have believed that, only a few hours earlier, the entire place was being battered by wind and rain, and in the most terrible confusion; of course, the general appearance of things—the street, the houses, and the stores—was more than enough to make you know that there had been, in fact, a fantastic hurricane.

'Look over there, Joe,' Papa said, pointing to a lamp-post. 'If you hadn't seen it for yourself, you wouldn't have believed it, would you?'

When I looked at the lamp-post, I saw that it was covered with a very thick coating of mud, grass roots, stems, leaves, and scraps of paper. It reminded me of a creature from outer space in a science-fiction film.

We had to be careful how we walked along the pavement because of the many trailing electric cables which were dangling from broken poles on both sides of the street.

'D'you think they are live?' I asked Papa.

'Shouldn't have thought so, son. The power ought to have been turned off by now. Anyway, let's not try to find out for ourselves, eh?'

We smiled at each other.

Then we started gazing at the extent of the damage to the houses along the street. It was very serious. We saw smashed windows, roofless houses, cracked concrete-work, broken veranda chairs, uprooted trees, twisted and splintered fences, and lots more.

We saw dead animals of all sorts. We saw washed-up motor-cars, bicycles, tricycles, handcarts, and other vehicles. Some of them were badly dented; all of them were spattered with layers of muck and mud.

When we got to Torrington Bridge, we immediately noticed that a whole section of it had been torn away. The iron rods, which are normally put into the concrete-mixture as supports, were bare and mangled and jutting out like long, thin fingers pointing in many directions. They looked, to me at any rate, like the tentacles of a giant octopus, partly spread out over the gully behind the bridge, and partly clawing at the people who were passing by on the pavement.

I must confess that I was surprised that there weren't many

people around. Those who were looked damp and tired.

Strange as it may seem, just at that moment Papa and I heard someone call my name, then another voice did so, and right after that we heard a ragged chorus of voices shouting, 'Joe! Joe! Caught up with you! Wait for us! Joe!'

I looked round, and there they were, all seven of them, running towards us: B.B. Perkins, Pants Martin, Four Eyes Dodd, Popeye Mason, Shaved Head Chin, Moon Face Smith, and Jiji-Wappie Haughton.

Papa smiled and made way for them. To me, he seemed more to be trying to avoid their stampede than to be stepping aside merely out of fatherly courtesy for his son's friends.

They rushed down on me, spinning me round and round, firing questions left and right, and giving me no time at all to reply to them. Generally, they were all asking how I had made out. Was I all right? Were my parents all right? Was my sister all right? Was my house all right? Where was I going? Did I know that—?

'What?' I asked B.B. 'Do I know what?'

B.B. was the only one calm enough to be able to answer me.

'Did you know that a certain laughing friend of ours, the original fearless one, was the only one of us who—' B.B.'s voice was drowned by a great burst of laughter from the others.

'The only one of us who *what*, B.B.?' I asked after the commotion had died down.

'Who was actually dead scared last night,' B.B. said.

'You don't mean Jiji?' I asked B.B.

'Yes.'

'Jiji who told me on the phone that the hurricane was nothing more than a Met. Office stunt?'

'Yes,' B.B. said.

'Jiji who said that the whole thing was a conspiracy to stop us from going to Carib?' I went on.

'Yes. That's our Jiji-Wappie.'

The boys started up again, laughing louder this time.

Papa began walking slowly away.

Jiji stepped forward to explain.

'Joe, boy,' he said, coming nearer and pleading with his arms extended, 'things were bad round my way. Fantastic, in fact. You should have been in our place at the height of the storm. The house was rocking like a boat and water was pouring in from all sides, even through the light switches and the sockets in the ceiling.'

'So, you were scared, were you?' I asked, mocking him slightly.

'Weren't you?' he asked pathetically.

'But you're the Great Laughing Man, Jiji, boy,' I teased.

'Fantastic, Joe,' was all Jiji said and stepped back among the others.

'By the way, Shaved Head, what happened to you?' I asked, hoping to shift the attention away from Jiji who was fidgeting a little and hanging his head.

'Nothing,' Shaved Head said shyly. 'Why d'you ask?'

'Tried to get you on the phone,' I explained. 'It rang and rang for ages. I tried again. And nothing. Weren't you at home?'

The boys were silent. We all knew how it was with Shaved Head. I suddenly remembered that he might cry or do something like it.

'Tell him you weren't answering the phone,' Popeye, the famous shadow-boxer, advised Shaved Head. 'Tell him you weren't in the mood for silly telephone conversations.'

'But what about your parents? Weren't they at home?' I pressed.

Shaved Head chuckled, lowered his head, and said, 'Of course we were all at home. It's just that Daddy had decided that he didn't want to be disturbed and that he didn't want

Mother talking for hours on end to any of her friends. So—'
He paused and chuckled again.

'So?' I urged him on.

'You do know where our phone is, don't you?' he asked me.

'Yes. Exactly where mine is at home. On the sideboard in the dining-room.'

'Well, Daddy opened one of the top drawers, put the phone inside it, pressed a cushion down on it, locked the drawer, and hid the key.'

We all laughed. So did Shaved Head.

The Cry Baby had made it at last, I thought.

I looked towards Papa and he was laughing too.

'By the way, Popeye, how are the guinea-pigs?' I asked, secretly hoping that nothing had happened to them.

'A stroke of good luck, boy,' Popeye began. 'I sneaked them into the house without permission and put them under my bed. My Uncle Ralph found them but I was allowed to keep them there.'

'What about you?' I asked Pants. 'Did you shoot at the Eye?'

'Clean through the centre with a Pants Special,' he boasted good-humouredly.

'Didn't drop dead, though,' Four Eyes jeered.

'How could it,' Pants hit back, 'when you, Mr. Four Eyes, were so terrified of the thing. Did you really expect the Eye to drop dead without the right kind of background music?'

We clapped loudly and imitated the sort of hurricane music we knew Four Eyes would have supplied at Carib. He took our teasing so well that after a while he too joined in, managing to drown all our combined attempts with the most fabulous crescendo you've ever heard.

Just then, Papa moved away and began talking to two men who had been listening to us and frowning their disapproval.

One of the men shouted, 'Why your parents have let you

82

noisy rascals out only God knows! Give me the hurricane any time!'

The other man added, 'And watch out for the live wires and the other bits and pieces of rubble. It's much too dangerous for you boys to be out in the street.'

'No danger at all,' B.B. said flatly, shaking his head full of grave knowledge and enormous technical facts. 'All the current has been turned off at the power plant. The wires aren't live. Besides, we aren't that silly to be running headlong into trouble without thinking about the consequences.'

That was that.

B.B. had spoken for all of us. Papa and the two men turned away, mumbling something about 'this modern generation'.

The only person whom we had not heard from up to now had been Moon Face Smith.

I noticed how unusually subdued he had been throughout, even though he had laughed along with the rest of us and had not seemed particularly worried by the hurricane.

But Moon Face was the Great Shouter. And as such, he hadn't lived up to his name, or even tried to so far.

It was his turn to report.

'Right, Moon Face, what's the score with you?' I asked.

'Nothing really,' he said casually, too casually for my liking.

'A fantastic night, eh?' I hinted broadly.

' 'Suppose so,' he said.

Very strange for Moon Face, I thought: after all, he must have been in his element what with all those thunderclaps and flashes of lightning the night before.

'You must have had bags of opportunity to shout encouragement, Moon Face, didn't you?' I asked, immediately realizing that the others were reacting peculiarly. They had gone absolutely still.

'Didn't,' Moon Face said. 'Nothing to encourage, boy.'

'I don't understand,' I said aimlessly.

83

'Moon Face got it in the neck,' Popeye explained.

'Got what?' I asked.

'His house,' Popeye said.

'How?' I must have sounded like a prize idiot, shouting when no one else was.

'You know we're up at Mona Heights, don't you?' Moon Face began. 'Well, our house cracked up early on. The walls caved in at the back of the house, and part of the ceiling blew off shortly afterwards. As a matter of fact, it happened long before the hurricane actually got going in earnest. Lucky for us, if you ask me.'

'So, what's the position?' I asked.

'Good timing really,' he said calmly. 'We all packed a few things and my father took us down to the Relief Centre at Coke Chapel.'

'From Mona to Coke Chapel—but, even by car, that's a long way. And dangerous too,' I said. 'What if the maximum strength of the hurricane had caught you half-way there?'

'Father drove like greased lightning, man!' He smiled.

'But why go to a relief centre so far away from Mona. And, anyway, how could they help you? They stock blankets and soup and that sort of thing. They didn't have space to put you up, did they?'

'Ah! that's what you think,' he said. 'The Red Cross man in charge of the Centre is a good friend—Father's friend. He gave us shelter in his own house in town. Not too far away from your place, Joe.'

'Have you heard anything about the house at Mona?'

'No. Smashed up, I imagine.'

I thought about our own new house on Tuna Avenue in Harbour View, the one that Mama and Papa were making plans to move into soon.

Quite suddenly, I wanted to leave the boys and continue my walk with Papa. I wanted to talk to him. I was worried about our new house. For after all, Harbour View faces the sea, and what's even worse, it's way above sea-level.

I imagined the full force of the wind breaking against the hill-side on which the Harbour View estate is built. I saw the damage before my very eyes: our new house, which wasn't even *our* house yet, completely demolished.

I said good-bye to the boys, promising to get in touch with them later on and trying not to show my anxiety. Had I, they would not have understood. And as usual, they would have laughed and made fun of me.

I went over to Papa. He nodded to the two men and held my shoulder.

We walked up Slipe Road and the scene was much the same. The shops and stores had all taken a bad beating from the wind. The pitch-pine frontages were soggy and water-marked. Those that weren't, looked chopped and scarred in parts. The concrete sections were washed by the rain to a whitish grey. In fact, all the buildings looked broken, bleached, and raw.

Papa and I had to kick a number of sprawling twigs and tree-branches out of the way as we headed towards Cross Roads. We noticed chunky streaks of fine weeds and tiny leaves wedged straight up the cracks between wooden fences, between closed double doors, and between other very narrow spaces. The weeds and leaves had been blown there, no doubt, by the regular riveting of the wind, and had been held in place by the constant pasting from the slanting rain. For a few seconds I closed my eyes and forced myself to listen to the *rat-tat-tat* of the hurricane as it machine-gunned its way through the cracks.

However, I ran right into an overturned dustbin and had to open my eyes again. Papa gave me a suspicious look. I grinned and caught up with him.

Cross Roads was like a ghost town. The criss-cross of the

overlapping roads was lined with thick helter-skelter patterns of sand and gravel, mud and grass, and a mixture of small driftwood and garbage.

'Could we go over to Harbour View, Papa?' I asked without warning, knowing that I would stand a chance of success if the idea took him by surprise.

'What for, Joe?' he asked, a little startled at the seriousness in my voice.

'We would be able to see how the house stood up to last night's beating, wouldn't we?'

'That's an idea, Joe. But how do we get there from here?' He paused. 'All right, don't mention it. You may have the strength to do it, but I'm *not* walking.'

We smiled.

The taxi driver drove slowly the whole way out to Harbour View, picking his way as carefully as the boys and I have had to when we're walking without shoes over the scorching sand at the sea-side.

He stopped just outside the house on Tuna Avenue, and Papa and I stared at it, not for once believing our eyes. We got out of the taxi, told the driver to wait for us, and stood gaping.

'Yours?' the man asked.

'What's left of it,' Papa said.

'Well, you know what they say: houses facing the sea always get a rough time; when they're on a hill and facing the sea— worse yet.' The driver continued, 'Good thing you weren't living in it.'

'True,' Papa said quietly.

I felt extremely sorry for him.

Like most of the others on the Avenue, our new house was wrecked, and what was more, it had all happened just a little before we and the other people were to take possession.

I did not know what to say to Papa, I merely stood beside him and gazed through the large holes and long gashes in the house. It looked like a giant birdcage.

We got back into the taxi and Papa asked the driver to take us to Cross Roads. He said something about wanting to walk home from Cross Roads because he felt the air might do him good.

On the way back, I reminded him: 'Big men don't cry, Papa.'

'I know, son,' he said softly, 'they plan.'

When we got to Cross Roads, we walked about for a while and looked once more at the damage and disorder, spread out everywhere.

'We've seen enough, haven't we, Joe?' Papa suggested, holding my shoulder and squeezing it lightly. 'We'd better turn back now, eh?'

'D'you think anybody got washed away?' I asked, not actually knowing why I had.

'I don't suppose we'll know until the report comes out in the *Gleaner*.'

'But what do *you* personally think, Papa?'

'One or two people might have been a little careless, son. You can never tell, can you? Besides, it was quite a hurricane, you know. The worst I've ever been through.'

There was a touch of real sadness in Papa's voice. It made me think of the damage to our house on Orange Street, the work-room, and, in particular, of the loss of the house on Tuna Avenue.

'Right, Joe,' Papa said brightly, clapping his hands together and rubbing them briskly, 'homeward bound.'

We turned round and there was Carib standing brazenly and undamaged before us. It was as it always is, big, broad, and solid. In some mysterious way, it seemed brilliantly whiter than usual, scrubbed, obviously, like everything else, by the powerful rainstorm.

'Oh, by the way,' Papa said, as we started back down Slipe Road, 'if good old Westmoreland is still on the map, I'd imagine that you and your sister might go down and stay with Aunt Maud until we get things fixed up properly at home. What d'you say to that?'

'If she's still on the map,' I agreed readily. 'Great!'

Papa looked down at me, smiled and said, 'If I know your Aunt Maud, she'll be there all right.'

GLOSSARY

THE GLEANER

The *Daily Gleaner* is Jamaica's leading newspaper, published in Kingston, the capital city.

ACKEE

The *ackee* is a delicious 'vegetable-fruit'. It has a thick, red outer skin and three or four yellow, fleshy pods with shiny, black seeds. When the pods are cooked, they taste somewhat like the yolk of a hard-boiled egg mashed with butter.

CARIB THEATRE

The Carib is the largest cinema in the West Indies. Cinemas are generally called 'theatres' in Jamaica. Many of them are open-air and some offer drive-in facilities. The Carib is not an open-air cinema.

MOSIED ALONG

To mosey along is an expression often used in Western stories to describe the leisurely walk of a confident cowboy.

THE NUMBER ELEVEN MANGO

A large, very sweet, juicy variety of Jamaican fruit. It is round and kidney-shaped. When ripe, the outer skin is yellowish-green, and the stringy pulp, which surrounds a hard single seed, is golden-yellow. How this particular mango got its name is not known.

MENTO

The *mento* is a certain type of Jamaican folksong. It is Jamaica's equivalent of the Trinidadian calypso. The calypso is usually topical, witty, and composed while being sung in front of a large audience, often in a Calypso Tent at Carnival time in February. The *mento*, on the other hand, is traditional, less popular (that is, in the modern popular musical sense), and it is sung more frequently in the country districts than it is in the towns and the city.